## "Who has a key t[...]"

"An assistant I share with Judge Rodriquez and maintenance. You think it was one of them?"

"No, there were fresh scratch marks on the lock. He risked breaking into your office for some reason. What was it?"

Aubrey made her way around to the other side of her desk. Sean started to rise, and she quickly said, "You stay there. If I need you, I'll let you know." She opened the top left drawer. "After I've gone through my office, I'll drive your car and take you to the ER to make sure you're okay."

He opened his mouth to reply.

She held up her palm. "No arguments on that. If something is wrong and you didn't get help, it would be my fault." She shut the top drawer and reached for the bottom one.

Their gazes clashed. A war of emotions played across his face while Aubrey pulled the second compartment out.

A rattling sound sent shivers down her body as she stared at the coiled rattlesnake, poised to strike.

**Margaret Daley**, an award-winning author of ninety books (five million sold worldwide), has been married for over forty years and is a firm believer in romance and love. When she isn't traveling, she's writing love stories, often with a suspense thread, and corralling her three cats, who think they rule her household. To find out more about Margaret, visit her website at margaretdaley.com.

Visit the Author Profile page at Harlequin.com for more titles.

# LONE STAR STANDOFF

## MARGARET DALEY

(H) HARLEQUIN® LOVE INSPIRED® SUSPENSE

If you purchased this book without a cover you should be aware
that this book is stolen property. It was reported as "unsold and
destroyed" to the publisher, and neither the author nor the
publisher has received any payment for this "stripped book."

Recycling programs
for this product may
not exist in your area.

 LOVE INSPIRED BOOKS

ISBN-13: 978-1-335-23208-3

Lone Star Standoff

Copyright © 2019 by Margaret Daley

All rights reserved. Except for use in any review, the reproduction
or utilization of this work in whole or in part in any form by any
electronic, mechanical or other means, now known or hereafter
invented, including xerography, photocopying and recording, or in
any information storage or retrieval system, is forbidden without
the written permission of the editorial office, Love Inspired Books,
195 Broadway, New York, NY 10007 U.S.A.

This is a work of fiction. Names, characters, places and incidents are
either the product of the author's imagination or are used fictitiously, and
any resemblance to actual persons, living or dead, business establishments,
events or locales is entirely coincidental.

This edition published by arrangement with Love Inspired Books.

® and TM are trademarks of Love Inspired Books, used under license.
Trademarks indicated with ® are registered in the United States Patent
and Trademark Office, the Canadian Intellectual Property Office and in
other countries.

www.Harlequin.com

Printed in U.S.A.

God is our refuge and strength,
a very present help in trouble.
–*Psalms* 46:1

To my mother-in-law, Marcella,
who has been a great supporter of my writing.

# ONE

District Judge Aubrey Madison left her office at the courthouse, her brain pounding against her skull. The jury was finally chosen today in her current trial—a trial that could propel her into the limelight, a place she'd rather not be. At least for the weekend, she could relax and enjoy time with her twins. They meant everything to her.

"Good night, Bill," she said to the deputy sheriff at the rear entrance.

"Judge Madison, I'll walk you out tonight."

"I appreciate the offer, but you need to guard the door."

He smiled. "I know. Part of the extra security for the Villa trial. I can keep an eye on the entrance and walk you to your car."

Aubrey sighed. Bill took his job seriously. "I know. That's why I parked near the entrance, so you wouldn't have to go so far." She stepped outside, where the sunset painted the sky with beautiful shades of red and yellow. "How are you doing?"

He slowed his pace, his forehead wrinkled. "I guess okay, Judge Madison."

She stopped and turned toward Bill, a large man with a slight potbelly. "I know what you're going through. My husband died two years ago. I'm here if you need to talk about your wife's death."

"Thanks." His face tensed, and he started walking again. "You have enough to deal with."

At the end of the sidewalk to the parking lot, Aubrey glanced at Bill. "I can take it from here. My car is right over there."

The deputy sheriff scanned the area then nodded.

She strolled the short distance to her car. The warmth from the spring day had already faded, and the chill in the air made her shiver. She slid behind the steering wheel and pulled out of her parking space. As she headed toward the exit of the lot behind the courthouse, reserved for people who worked inside, she passed Bill and waved.

When she arrived home a short time later, she punched the garage-door opener then drove inside and parked next to her mother's car. She didn't know what she would have done if her mama hadn't insisted on coming to stay with her at least until Camy and Sammy went to elementary school. Two years ago when her husband was murdered, Aubrey had to go back to work because of Samuel's sudden death. Their savings had all been wiped out by medical bills when the twins were born early. She'd always intended to return to work, but not until they were in elementary school. Instead she'd run for the judge position six months later.

Not wanting to dwell on a past she couldn't change, she hurried into the house, the scent of beef and onions permeating the place. "What's for dinner? It smells great."

Her mother pulled out a casserole dish from the oven and set it on a burner. "My lasagna. Camy and Sammy helped me."

"Where are they?" Aubrey wondered how messy the kitchen had been after her twins' "help."

"When I heard your car pull into the garage, I had them go wash their hands. How did it go today?"

"Long, but the two attorneys have finally settled on a jury."

"Just in time for the weekend." Her mother brushed a stray strand of black hair behind her ear.

"Yes. I threatened to continue late into the night if they didn't." Aubrey put her briefcase and purse on the desk nearby. "I'd better go check on my kids. It's too quiet. They've had enough time to wash their hands."

Aubrey left the kitchen and walked upstairs and down the hallway toward her twins' bedrooms at the end. The light from the bathroom beckoned her. Giggles resonated down the corridor. That sound usually meant she would have to spend time cleaning up whatever mess her rascals had made. She hurried her steps.

When she entered the bathroom, she looked down at the puddle of water the twins were standing in. She stared at Camy and Sammy, drenched from head to toe. She pressed her lips together, suppressing the laugh at the sight of her soggy children. That would only encourage them. "Who won the battle?"

They each pointed at themselves.

"Who started it?" Aubrey asked, trying to put on her stern face.

"He started it," her daughter immediately said.

"I dinna." Sammy stomped his foot, and water on the floor went flying, hitting Aubrey's pants.

After the serious day she'd had in court, her children's antics actually lightened her mood. She still fought her smile and remained calm. "Don't move." She marched down the hall to the linen closet and grabbed several bath towels, then returned to her children, still standing where she'd left them. Even though they were twins, they were like night and day. Camy had dark hair and eyes like Aubrey and her mother, while Sammy took after his father's side with light brown hair and hazel eyes.

She gave each child a towel. "Mop the floor with these then put them in the tub." Leaning her shoulder against the doorjamb with her arms crossed, she watched her four-year-olds do the best job they could. When they finished, she stepped to the side. "Put on some dry clothes, then bring the wet ones back here and place them in the tub, too."

Heads down, the twins left the bathroom.

After they disappeared into their bedrooms, she completed the cleanup, then headed back to the kitchen.

"What happened?" Her mama brought the casserole dish to the table and set it down on a hot pad.

"The usual. No doubt the water fight started out innocently but quickly morphed into an all-out battle. They're changing clothes." A moment later Sammy came into the room with a ragged T-shirt on backward. She refrained from saying anything, but the sight of what he was wearing reminded her of what she'd done at lunch today. She snatched up her keys and headed for the door to the garage in the utility room. "I forgot something in the trunk of my car."

When she stepped into the garage, a faint rotting odor wafted to her. She neared the large trashcan and lifted the top. It was empty because the garbage had been picked up earlier that day. But as she neared the rear of her car, the smell grew stronger. She clicked the car trunk's button on her key fob, and the lid popped up. The nauseating scent engulfed her. She looked down at a large, dead brown rat lying next to a shopping bag from the store she'd visited at lunchtime.

She froze. The dead rat definitely hadn't been there earlier today. Rats and snakes were her two fears. How did it get into her trunk? When was it put there? And *why*?

Fear blanketed her as she thought of her current trial—a top drug cartel lieutenant faced a first-degree murder charge.

Texas Ranger Sean McNair entered his house and tossed his car keys into a bowl in his kitchen near the door to the garage. Another shipment of drugs had slipped through his fingers today. He felt it in his gut. His tip hadn't paid off. He was too late to stop the drugs from coming into the United States, and his recent suspicions about the Port Bliss Police Department had been confirmed. Someone had warned the Coastal Cartel about the raid.

He made his way to his deck overlooking the water between the Texas mainland and South Padre Island. Gripping the railing, he leaned against it, relishing the cool, late-spring breeze laced with the scent of the sea that always calmed his frustration. A seagull flew over Sean's home, heading for the island.

Frustration churned his stomach. He was one of three people covering a large area of the southernmost tip of the state. Everything pointed to a cartel thug murdering the Texas Ranger before him, but he had no concrete evidence to prove the case. The fallen Texas Ranger had a wife and two babies—who were left without a father. He hadn't known Samuel Madison other than by his reputation of being a good law enforcement officer. When Sean had been moved to Company D to replace the slain fellow officer, he'd met the man's wife. The look of despair in her dark brown eyes still haunted him, even after two years.

He'd asked to be transferred, especially with the Coastal Cartel firming its base of operation in the area over the past few years. Someone in the cartel was responsible for his brother's disappearance. In his gut, he knew that Jack was dead. But he and his family needed closure on what had happened to him.

Sean had slowly been digging into the organization to finally bring it down. It wouldn't return his younger brother, but if he could destroy it, the cartel henchman wouldn't be able to tear apart another family like his had been. His mother had never recovered from Jack's tailspin into the drug world that ultimately killed him. There had been nothing he could do to stop his little brother. Jack had been living in Port Bliss for the past four years while Sean had been a Texas Highway Patrol officer clear across the state in Amarillo, where they had grown up.

Sean took a deep, cleansing breath of the sea-laced air, closing his eyes as he tried to forget the description of Jack's apartment two years ago when he went missing. Blood everywhere but no body.

The sound of his cell phone's ringtone intruded into his thoughts. He started to ignore it, then with a glance at the screen, he changed his mind and quickly answered. "Hello. Is something wrong?" He'd told Aubrey Madison to call him if she ever needed his help, because her husband's killer had never been brought in, either. This was the first time she had.

"There may be a problem."

"May?"

"Someone left a dead rat in the trunk of my car, and I think it could be connected to the trial I'm currently the judge on."

A rat was often left at a scene where the cartel went after someone. There had been one in Jack's apartment. "Bento Villa's trial?"

"Yes." Aubrey's voice quavered, reminding him of the times he'd interviewed her about her husband and had worked with her to find the killer. They had both being grieving at that time, although he'd never told her about Jack's case. He'd even wondered if his brother's disappearance had been connected to her husband's death somehow. The incidents were days apart. "Have you called the police?"

"Not yet."

"Don't. I'll be there in twenty minutes." *Even if I have to break a few speeding laws.* "Leave the rat where it is. Go inside and lock the doors until I get there. Do you have a gun and know how to use it?" Sean entered his house and snatched up his keys.

"Yes, it was my husband's."

"Good. Get it just in case." With what he'd seen working this area over the past two years, a dead rat was not only used as a symbol of the cartel but also to send a message they would always follow up. Suddenly a question popped into Sean's mind: Was the dead rat a warning to the judge that the cartel was coming after her?

"Okay. Thank you." The judge disconnected their call.

He stuffed his phone into his pocket and left his bungalow. As the sun disappeared totally below the horizon, he sped as fast as he could toward her house in the next town.

Aubrey slammed the trunk down, her stomach roiling as the rotting odor grew worse by the minute. She hurried into the house and went immediately to the safe for the revolver she'd kept more as a memory of her husband than in the expectation she would ever use it, even though she knew how to fire a gun and keep it serviceable. But she had her children and mother to think about and protect. She hid the weapon in the big pocket of a bulky sweater she donned.

She returned to the kitchen, where her mother sat at the table with Camy and Sammy, waiting for her. Mama glanced at her bulging sweater pocket and furrowed her brows. She started to say something, but Aubrey quickly shook her head. She sat, but didn't know if she could eat much. Her nausea persisted while her heartbeat raced. She couldn't get it out of her mind that the rat was a warning.

"Let's bless the food," Aubrey said. "Sammy, it's your turn."

Her son joined hands with her and his sister, then bowed his head. "Thanks for the food and my *madre* and *abuela*." He looked up then hurriedly added, "And Camy."

Aubrey smiled at the Spanish words her son loved

to throw in. Her mother was working with the twins to teach them her family's language as well as English.

Her daughter turned her head so fast her long black ponytail swung around. "I cleaned up more than Sammy."

"No, you dinna."

Aubrey gave each twin a long stare, then replied, "What's the rule when we're eating?"

"No fighting," they both said.

Aubrey ignored Camy sticking out her tongue at Sammy and instead stared at the food on her plate, wondering how she was going to eat it all. She checked her watch. The Texas Ranger who'd taken her husband's place should be here soon. How was she going to keep her worries from affecting her children? She'd been on the bench for almost two years and even dealt with a few drug cases involving low-level members of the Coastal Cartel. Nothing had happened during that time. Was the message in her car trunk because the man on trial was one of the lieutenants in the cartel?

"Mama!"

Aubrey blinked and glanced at her daughter. "What?"

"Are ya lost in your mind?"

"Huh?"

"I've been askin' ya for more *leche*." Camy held up her empty glass. "I'll pour it."

"No!" The last time her daughter had tried to refill her milk, it went everywhere. "Sorry. I was lost in thought." Aubrey took the glass from Camy and crossed to the refrigerator.

When she came back to the table, she intercepted a puzzled look from her mother. She didn't want to say anything in front of her children, so she switched her attention to Camy and forced a grin. As she started to sit again, the doorbell rang.

Aubrey jerked to a standing position. "I'll get it. I may be a while. It's work. Finish your dinner. I'll eat later."

Her mama stared at her for a few seconds, then said to the twins, "After dinner, you two can help me with the dishes, and then we can play a game."

A resounding cheer came from her children as Aubrey rushed toward the entry hall and reached to clasp the knob. She stopped in mid-motion. Instead she looked through the peephole and saw it was Texas Ranger McNair, then opened the door. "Thank you for coming." She stepped to the side for him to enter.

She hadn't seen him at the courthouse in over a month and had forgotten how tall and well built he was. Dressed in a long-sleeved white shirt with a striped gray-and-red tie, black pants, an off-white cowboy hat, brown boots and his badge pinned over his heart, he had a commanding air about him. The sight of him dressed for work reminded her of her husband, and a knot clogged her throat. That first year after Samuel's murder, she saw Sean a couple of times a week while he worked the case.

He paused a few feet from her, turned toward her and held out his hand. "It's nice to see you again." His dark blue eyes roamed over her features, and a slow smile spread across his tanned face. "Although I wish it were under different circumstances."

She shook his hand. "I agree, Sean. I have a home office where we can talk. My children are in the kitchen, and I don't want them to overhear our conversation."

"I understand. Lead the way."

Aubrey passed him in the foyer, feeling dwarfed by his large frame. She was only five four while he must be at least six and a half feet, if not more. She waved her hand toward a brown leather love seat and two chairs. Although she had a desk, she usually ended up working on the two-cushion couch with her laptop and papers spread all over the coffee table.

"When I'm not in a trial, I often work from home to be here for my two kids. It helps that my mother lives with me, and I'm only ten minutes away from the courthouse."

While he took a chair, she sat on the love seat, thinking they should switch places. He looked so big in the wingback. He took off his hat and laid it on the coffee table between them, then ran his fingers through his thick, short black hair. "Being the judge in the Bento Villa trial must be tough."

"Yes, it's taken days to find a jury. The trial will actually start on Monday. When you leave, I'll open the garage door and show you the dead rat in my car's trunk. I didn't touch it. In fact, I left a shopping bag in there with clothes I bought at lunch for my twins, Sammy and Camy. They're four and a half. My mama takes care of them when I'm working." When she and Sean had talked before, it had been centered on her husband's case, but if someone was coming after her now, Sean needed to know everything about her family. They could be affected, too.

"Is your son named after his dad?"

"Yes, and Camy after my mama. Her name is Camilla." Texas Ranger McNair had always been easy to talk to. Aubrey reclined back, trying to relax some of her tight muscles that had stayed with her since she left the courthouse. The only place she dealt with her job at home was in this office. When she walked out of here, her family became her focus—until someone had left that message in her trunk. "A dead rat has been used by the cartel before as a warning. I've also received a few hang-ups at my office in the courthouse since I was assigned to the Villa trial."

"Have you received calls like that at other times?"

"Occasionally, and that's why I shrugged them off this time. I know it's not Bento himself, since he's in jail and his communications are monitored. But the Coastal Cartel is big and ruthless."

"What's the security for this trial?"

"Extra guards at the courthouse and inside where the trial is. I've always felt safe at work. Someone coming after me won't change the fact that Bento Villa is on trial for the murder of Hector Martin."

"This is a high-profile case." Sean wrote something on the pad he held. "Can we narrow down the time and place where the rat could have been put in your trunk? Then I can check security cameras to see if I can catch the person on tape."

"During lunch, I usually eat in my office at the courthouse, but today I needed to get away. The atmosphere is tense. Since we were getting near the end of the selection of jurors, I announced a two-hour lunch period. I still ate in my office and decided to lie down on the couch and take a nap. Since this case began, I haven't slept as well as I usually do. But I couldn't fall asleep. So I decided to go shopping for summer clothes for the kids. The dead rat wasn't in the trunk when I put that bag in there after visiting the store I usually get their clothes at."

"What store?"

"Clothes Galore on Main Street."

"Did you go right back to the courthouse?"

Aubrey looked away from Sean's intense gaze. "No. I went to Sweet Haven Parlor and had a double scoop of cookie-dough ice cream in a waffle cone. Indulging always manages to cheer me up."

He chuckled. "I've been there before. Their ice cream is great."

"What flavor?" He made her feel at ease during this tense time.

"Chocolate. Don't tell anyone that's my weakness."

She laughed. The sound surprised her even more. For the past thirty minutes, she'd been tied in knots, and in a brief time he'd gotten her to laugh. But she quickly sobered as he wrote on his pad. This visit was about someone leaving her a message. She couldn't take that lightly.

"I'll check the security cameras at the courthouse and Sweet Haven Parlor, if they have any. Did you go anywhere else?"

"No. I came right back and had only a few minutes to get to my office and put on my robe."

"When you drove home from the courthouse, did you stop anywhere and leave your car unattended?"

"No. After this week, all I wanted to do was get home."

Sean stood and pocketed his notepad. "Show me your car."

"Let's go out front. I'll raise the garage door. If we go through the kitchen, my children will want to come with us. They're curious and ask so many questions." They reminded her of her husband in that way. He'd always proclaimed that was what made him a good investigator—and what had probably led to his death. She shivered at the thought.

As she exited her office, laughter from the kitchen drifted to her. She smiled. No doubt Sammy and Camy were competing at clearing the dishes from the table.

"Your kids sound like they're having fun." Sean opened the front door.

"They love to compete with each other but are quick to stand up for one another when needed." Aubrey put in her code on the pad at the garage. The noise of the door rising filled the quiet. She hoped her kids didn't get curious at hearing the sound and want to check it out.

As she approached the rear of her car, she popped the trunk. The odor of the dead rat overwhelmed her even more than before. Shivering at the sight, she pinched her nose and gestured toward the rat.

Sean took pictures of it then put on gloves to handle the rat. "I need something to put this in. Can I use the bag your children's clothes are in?"

"Sure." She moved toward Sean and picked up the bag to remove the outfits. As she pulled them out, something dropped onto the concrete. She heard it before she saw what came out of the bag. Clutching the clothes against her chest, she intended to kneel and pick up whatever fell.

"I'll get it." After putting the bag with the rat on the floor, Sean squatted and reached under the vehicle. When he stood, he held his palm out flat toward Aubrey.

She stared at her husband's hammered-gold wedding band with her name engraved in it. It had been missing since his murder.

The twins' outfits fell to the concrete as her legs gave out.

# TWO

Sean quickly clasped Aubrey's upper arms and held her upright. Her wide, dark brown eyes stared through him while color drained from her beautiful face and her short dark hair lay in contrast to her pale skin. "What's wrong?"

She shuddered, opening her mouth for a few seconds but shutting it before saying anything. She took the ring from his palm. Tears glistened in her eyes. She closed them and inhaled a deep breath.

"Aubrey?"

She swiped a wet tear track from her cheek, straightened her shoulders and looked at him. "That's Samuel's wedding ring. When he was murdered, the killer took his ring. My name is engraved inside. I didn't think I would ever see it again, especially not among my children's clothes."

No wonder she was stunned. "So whoever left the rat was either your husband's killer or knew the guy."

"And neither is good news. Why now, after two years?"

"A connection between Villa's trial and Samuel's murder?"

"Possibly. Both involved drugs. Villa is a lieutenant of the Coastal Cartel." Aubrey held up the ring. "And they're sending me a message."

Sean glanced over his shoulder to where his SUV was parked in the driveway. Darkness had settled over the landscape. "Let's go inside and talk about this. What kind of security system do you have?"

"I have an alarm system with a couple of cameras inside, as well as motion detectors by the porch and garage."

"Any cameras outside?"

Aubrey shook her head then turned her attention in the same direction. "What if they're watching me?"

"You need to get a couple for the front and back-yard."

"I'll call my company tomorrow and arrange for them to add them as soon as they can."

Sean scooped up the clothes at their feet and gave them to her, then picked up the bag with the dead rat. "Go inside. I'm locking this in my vehicle, then we'll talk some more."

She nodded, but before she reached the garage entrance into the kitchen, a little boy with brown hair opened the door and poked his head out.

"Mama, I'm hiding from *Abuela*." Sammy clamped his gaze on Sean, and his eyes grew big.

"Let's get inside." Aubrey hustled her son into the house and waited for Sean to leave the garage before putting the door down. "I'll let you in at the front."

Sean hurried to his SUV, his gaze sweeping the terrain for anything unusual. He assessed several places where someone could possibly hide and watch Aubrey's house. Not only did he lock his rear door, but also the evidence box built into his car under the back mats. Then he headed for the porch and started to ring the bell.

Aubrey swung the door open before he could push the button. "I promised my son I would introduce you to him. He said you look like how his daddy looked in some of the pictures he's seen. I told him you were a Texas Ranger like his dad, and he got all excited. Do you mind?"

"Not at all." His older sister in Amarillo had two boys, ages seven and nine, as well as a five-year-old girl. He loved visiting them. "Where is he?"

"In the den with his sister and my mother." She closed and locked the door. "This way."

He followed Aubrey toward the back of the house, realizing he was over a foot taller than her.

Sammy stood in the entrance to the room with a big grin on his face. "Did ya know my daddy?"

"I met him once, but I really didn't know him. Everyone says he was a great Texas Ranger."

Sammy's grin grew even bigger. "That's what Mama says." The little boy grabbed Sean's hand and tugged him forward. "I gotta show ya somethin'."

Sean accompanied the child as they crossed the room to the fireplace. The boy pointed at the mantel to a photo of his father, wearing a long-sleeved white shirt with a blue tie and an off-white cowboy hat.

"He has on his badge like you. And we have it!" Sammy pulled on Sean's hand, guiding him to an end table with the star badge framed in a shadow box. "I'm gonna wear one when I grow up." He thrust out his chest.

"I felt that way when I was a young boy." Sean

turned toward the little girl standing next to Aubrey. "And you must be Camy."

She nodded but stepped closer to her mother. Seeing them side by side, he noted a strong resemblance between the two.

"She's shy with strangers," Sammy said.

Sean smiled and winked at Camy, whose eyes grew round as saucers.

"I'm Camilla Roberts, their grandma, or as Sammy has been saying lately, their *abuela*." The petite older woman with black hair and the same dark brown eyes as Aubrey stood and held her hand out.

Sean shook it. "It's nice to meet all of you."

"Camy and Sammy, it's time to get ready for bed." Camilla peered at her daughter. "The Texas Ranger is here to talk business with your mama."

While Camy went to her grandmother, Sammy stood still. "I'm not sleepy. I want to stay."

"Samuel Craig Madison, this isn't negotiable. Go with Grandma now." Aubrey's firm voice emphasized the word *now*, which drew a big frown from her son, but Sammy left with his grandmother.

"Sorry about that. My son takes his job as the man of the house very seriously. He thinks he's supposed to know about everything that goes on here. Let's go back to my office."

As they left the den, Sean said, "I understand. My father died when I was fourteen. I was the oldest male. I have two sisters, one younger and one older, and a younger brother. I thought I needed to protect them and be the man of the house, too." Yet he hadn't been able to protect his youngest sibling. He'd failed to accomplish his dad's last request.

"Sammy's only four and a half. He got that idea from a kid at church about six months ago."

"Kids are growing up too fast today."

"You don't have to tell this mother." Aubrey walked toward the doorway. "I need to put these new clothes in the washing machine. The idea that someone might have handled them in addition to the faint odor of a dead rat are more than enough reasons to wash them before they wear them."

Sean glanced up and down the hallway before asking, "I wish you had answers to your husband's death. It's hard to get closure when there are so many unknowns. Do you mind telling me again about what happened? I haven't had a chance to work on his case for a couple of months." The influx of drugs had increased in the past few months, and he was determined to do what he could to stop the flow. He often wished there was more time in a day to do all he wanted. He'd even neglected Jack's missing-person case.

"Sure. Have you had dinner yet?"

"No. When you called, I'd just arrived home." He entered the kitchen.

"Knowing my mama, she put the leftovers in the refrigerator for me to have later. It won't take long to heat them up in the microwave. It's lasagna. Mama is a great cook, a trait I haven't inherited from her." She crossed to the utility room and disappeared inside.

Like the rest of the house, the kitchen was clean and neat, with little evidence they had just eaten dinner. He was glad that Aubrey had help with her children. He'd been there for his mother after his father died in a ranch accident. He'd tried his best to do what his dad had done at the family's ranch and go to high school, then later college. Being a parent was hard, but being a single one was even more difficult. Reflecting on Sammy showing him the picture of his father and his badge brought a smile to Sean's face. But then he remembered Camy's shyness, and he thought about his younger sister, who'd been a lot like Aubrey's daughter.

When Aubrey returned to the kitchen and opened the refrigerator, she shot him a look around the door. "Are you really hungry? There's a lot here."

He nodded. "I'm always really hungry when it's a home-cooked meal. Can I help?"

"Put this plate into the microwave on three and a half minutes, please." She gave him her meal with plastic wrap covering it.

Ten minutes later, they were seated across from each other at the table in the alcove. The aroma of lasagna teased his senses, but before digging in, he bowed his head and said a silent prayer for help from God in solving what was going on with the dead rat and Aubrey's husband's wedding ring. He didn't have a good feeling about this. Someone was playing games—possibly deadly ones—with her, and it was likely connected to the cartel.

When he looked up, their gazes connected. He realized she'd been praying, too. Sean took a bite of his dinner, savoring the delicious Italian dish. "Mmm. Tell your mom this is great."

Aubrey smiled. "I will. She loves to hear that. Once she thought about being a chef and having her own restaurant."

"Why didn't she?"

Her smile vanished. "My husband was killed. She

told me the deal fell through, but I've always wondered if that was the case."

"Speaking of your husband, tell me again what you recall about his death."

She scooped up a forkful of lasagna and ate it. "When he didn't come home from work, I tried getting in touch with him, and it went to voice mail. I left a message to call me. I thought I would get a return call, but as the night turned into the next day, I knew something was terribly wrong. Even before the kids were born, he always kept in regular touch with me throughout the day. I called the Weslaco office to see if they knew anything. They didn't but said they would look into it and get back to me. I then called the Port Bliss Police Department and reported my concerns. That day was the longest twenty-four hours I've ever gone through."

Around the time of her husband's death, Sean had received the notification of his brother's disappearance. When the police described Jack's destroyed apartment and the blood at the scene, he'd known his brother was probably killed, especially given some of the people he'd associated with. "Do you know what Samuel was working on? When I took over shortly after his death, I only found two open cases he'd been looking into."

"Which ones?" Aubrey reached for her iced tea.

"A shipment of guns missing and the disappearance of Jack McNair."

She stopped in mid-motion and looked toward him. "Any relationship to you?"

"My younger brother. Did Samuel ever talk about him? There wasn't a lot in the case file on his death." On the side, he'd been searching for any information on his missing brother and had come up empty. According to everyone he'd talked to, Jack just vanished one day.

"Not that I can remember. When Samuel died, everything got crazy. I felt for months that all I was doing was going through the motion of living. Attending his funeral was one of the hardest things I've done. The coffin was closed due to the grisly nature of the murder."

The pain in her expression and voice twisted Sean's gut. From the pictures of Jack's apartment, his little brother had been tortured, too. He wanted to know why. After two years of searching for answers, Sean hadn't come close to solving his death, nor Samuel Madison's.

"I couldn't even box up Samuel's possessions. Mama took care of that while I was trying to act like everything was all right for Camy's and Sammy's sakes and trying to keep up with two toddlers who didn't understand where their daddy was." She stared at her half-eaten lasagna for a long moment then lifted her head, looking right at him. "And now someone returned my husband's wedding ring. It doesn't make any sense. Why now?"

"If I knew that, I could figure out who killed him."

"I want justice for my husband, but dragging it all up again also brings pain."

"I know. I feel the same way about my younger brother." Sean finished the last bite of his lasagna. "I need to leave, but if you think of anything more I should know, please call me. And if you receive another threat, call immediately."

Aubrey rose and stacked his empty plate on hers. "I will. Should I notify the local police?"

He brought their glasses to the sink. "Yes, and the sheriff's office. The guards at the courthouse need to be aware of what happened. I'll be talking with the police chief and the sheriff about the incident. Tomorrow I'll go look at the security tapes to see if there's anyone acting suspicious. Also, I'll check at Sweet Haven. It'll give me a good reason to have a chocolate ice-cream cone. I might just have a triple-dip one. I haven't been there for months, not like someone I know." He grinned, winked and picked up his cowboy hat then set it on his head.

Aubrey accompanied him to the entry hall. "I appreciate you coming over. I wasn't sure what I should do."

He stepped out onto the porch and turned back to her. "Ma'am, it's my pleasure to help you." He tipped his cowboy hat then left her.

When he slid behind the steering wheel, he swung his attention to the front door. Aubrey still stood there, her petite body framed in the entrance. She had a reputation of being a tough judge, but at the moment there was nothing tough about her. Her vulnerability drew him to her.

As he drove away, he called the police chief. "Juan, I need a police car posted outside Judge Aubrey Madison's house."

"Why?"

Sean explained what had happened. "I'm looking into this threat, but with the trial she's overseeing, she should have someone escort her to and from the courthouse as a precaution for the time being."

"I'll have one out there right away."

"Thanks, Juan. I'll keep you up-to-date on what I find out."

"But you don't have a good feeling about this?"

"No." He thought about the recent cartel violence in the past few months. He was afraid Aubrey was caught up in the middle of what was going down. Bento Villa was the right-hand man for the head of the Coastal Cartel and like a son to Sanchez, who ran the whole organization from Mexico. Now the man was in jail and on trial for murder. And her husband's murder had no doubt been carried out by a cartel member or possibly Villa, a hands-on leader, according to his informant.

Saturday morning before everyone else was up, Aubrey made another cup of tea and sat at the table, staring out into the backyard at the bright sunlit day. She'd gone through the house and opened all the blinds over the windows on the sides and rear of the house. She kept the front ones closed because there was a patrol car parked in her driveway.

When Sean called her last night to tell her about the police officer assigned to guard her, she'd had mixed feelings. Sammy had told her on a number of occasions that he was going to be a police officer when he grew up—just like his daddy. Having a police officer around would keep that dream in the foreground for Sammy. She didn't want that for her son. She'd lost her husband to the job, and she didn't want to lose anyone else to it. She'd even prayed for the Lord to change his mind before he was an adult.

With this new trial, she didn't see any way around the protection. It had been a good move to have a police presence at her house to discourage anyone who wanted to do her harm. But she didn't want Sammy to know she could be in danger.

"There's police outside." Sammy ran into the kitchen, still in his pajamas, with the biggest smile on his face. "Can I go out and say hi?"

"No. You're in your pj's." Before she could say anything else, her son whirled around and raced out of the kitchen.

Aubrey started to go after him in case he decided to ignore what she said, but the sound of him stomping up the staircase stopped her. Most likely he was going upstairs to get dressed. She took a sip of tea then stood. Knowing Sammy, she headed for the entry hall and leaned back against the front door, arms crossed over her chest. Aubrey had left the alarm system on, and she didn't want her son to trigger it if he tried to sneak outside. Both her mother and daughter were still sleeping. And as expected, he came down the steps, wearing shorts, a T-shirt and cowboy boots.

He didn't notice her until she asked, "Where are you going?"

"To see if Brad can play."

*Sure, with a stop at the police car.* "It's too early, and you haven't had breakfast."

Sammy plopped down on the last step and frowned.

There was no way to hide the fact that a patrol car would be there for the time being. She didn't want to scare her son, but she couldn't ignore that she was being protected. "Tell you what. Let's both go eat a bowl of cereal, and then I'll get dressed and we'll go out front to say hi to the police officer."

Sammy jumped to his feet and ran toward the kitchen. Aubrey followed at a sedate pace, wishing she had her son's energy.

It was an hour later before Aubrey opened the front

door and her two kids raced outside and down the porch steps. She'd called the police to let the patrol officer know her kids wanted to meet him. She'd also received a text from Sean saying he was coming by, and he should be here soon. Heat suffused her face when she thought about the extra care she'd gone to when he texted her about seeing her today. She'd hurried back up the stairs and changed into a new pair of jeans and a white blouse instead of sweatpants and an old T-shirt.

While her twins sat in the front seat of the patrol car, the officer told them about the different things he did as a law enforcement officer. They got to turn on the red lights, but the young man stopped short of sounding the siren.

So intent on her children, she didn't realize that Sean had parked along the curb and approached her until he said in a soft voice right behind her, "One day I'll let them try the siren in my car."

Her heartbeat tripled its rate, leaving Aubrey sucking in shallow breaths. With a laptop bag slung over his shoulder, Sean moved to her side while the officer showed her kids the equipment in the trunk. Sammy was smiling from ear to ear while Camy began looking bored. Aubrey turned toward Sean. "Did you find out who put the rat in my car?"

"Not who, but at least where he did it, I believe. I went through all the surveillance tapes available last night and this morning. After talking to you, I left here and went to the courthouse to look at its surveillance tapes. Nothing happened in its parking lot that I could tell, but your vehicle was parked in a blind spot at Sweet Haven. I went by the ice-cream parlor first thing this morning. Their security cameras were focused on the front and back doors and inside the place, not the parking lot. They didn't show anything unusual. I've obtained traffic cam footage around the time you went to Sweet Haven and would like you to view it with me. The rat must have been placed in your trunk during the twenty minutes you were inside the ice-cream parlor. Did you notice a car following you when you left at lunchtime yesterday?"

"No, but I have to confess—" she paused, hating to admit she'd been careless "—I wasn't paying attention. I was relishing getting away from the courthouse for an hour. I've felt so confined since the Villa trial started."

"For a good reason. Bento Villa is high up in the Coastal Cartel and its drug ring component."

"He sure isn't cooperating with the prosecution. He was offered a good deal in exchange for information on the cartel. He refused it. Not that I thought he would take a deal." Thinking about the threat now hanging over her, she approached the police officer. "Sammy and Camy, it's time to go back inside. What do you say to Officer Carter?"

"Thank you," Sammy said in a loud voice that half the neighborhood probably heard, while Camy mumbled her thanks.

"I appreciate you doing this," Aubrey said then tried to corral her two children toward the front porch. Finally Sammy glued himself to Sean while Camy took Aubrey's hand and practically dragged her toward the house.

"Is your car like that?" Sammy asked Sean, slowing his pace.

Sean patted Sammy's shoulder and kept walking right behind Aubrey. "Similar."

Her son pointed to the top of Sean's SUV. "Where's your siren?"

"Inside the vehicle. I stick it on top if I need to."

At the bottom of the steps, Sammy's forehead winkled. "But no one will know you're a policeman."

Sean chuckled and proceeded up the steps to the porch. "Sometimes I don't want them to know."

Aubrey held the front door open. "Hurry up, Sammy, or the mosquitoes will invade the house. You know how much they love biting me."

"Me, too," Camy said and hurried into the house and down the hall toward the kitchen.

When everyone was inside, Aubrey shut the door and locked it. Her son remained next to Sean. "Sammy, I need to talk to him. Grandma is fixing breakfast."

He stuck out his bottom lip. "I already had cereal."

"That was to tide you over until Grandma got up to fix our big breakfast we have on Saturday as a family." Her mother also did it Sunday before church. She drew in a deep breath. "It smells like pancakes, probably chocolate chip."

Sammy took off for the kitchen.

"He has two speeds, fast or slow. Usually with no in between." Aubrey gestured toward her office. "We can talk in here."

Inside the room, she closed the door. "I appreciate your quick response on this. Anything I can do to help, I will. Let's look at the traffic cam footage. Maybe it'll jog my memory."

"I hope so." He made his way to the couch and sat. After he took out his laptop, she joined him on the love seat. Sitting next to him, only inches away, caused her heart to beat faster. A faint musky scent wafted to her as she tried to focus on the video.

"I'm starting when you left the courthouse, and we'll follow your trip as best as we can, since Port Bliss only has traffic cams in the downtown area and a few roads in and out of town."

The sight of a white sedan a couple of cars behind her while she drove from the clothing store to Sweet Haven nagged at her mind. When she drove into the parking lot on the side of the ice-cream parlor, the white car passed on by, not even slowing down. For the next twenty minutes, she kept expecting to see it, but she didn't.

"I thought for a moment the person in the white sedan might be following me, but it kept going."

"Why did you think that?"

"Because…" Her voice faded as she searched her mind, trying to remember why it had bothered her. Other cars had been behind her. Why that one?

Because the white car had been in the parking lot at the clothing store and pulled out into traffic when she left the shop—it was the only vehicle that started following her from there.

# THREE

Sean rewound the video footage, paused it and zoomed in on the white vehicle, trying to make out the license plate. The last three numbers were 249, but he couldn't make out the first part of it. "Is there something that makes you suspicious of that car?"

Aubrey sat back on the couch. "When I saw it on the screen, it provoked a memory. I don't remember seeing it when it was behind me. It was at least six cars back and hidden from my view in the rearview mirror. But when I left the parking lot at the clothing store, that white car pulled into it. The person must have turned around fast to be behind me when I went to Sweet Haven."

"Did you see the driver?"

"I glanced for maybe a second or two in that direction. The glass was tinted too dark to make out the driver."

"White is the most common color for a vehicle. What makes you think the one in the parking lot is the same car on this footage?"

"The driver's-side back fender has a dent in it." Aubrey leaned forward and tapped the computer screen. "There."

Sean focused onto the area she indicated. "It's a Chevy Malibu. So the driver must have turned around in the clothing store parking lot as you said and quickly pulled back out into the traffic. I'll follow up on this and see who owns the car."

She smiled. "I'm glad you could tell what make it was, because all I saw was a white car."

He chuckled. "It's a man thing." He punched the key to forward the video. "He didn't park near the Sweet Haven Parlor."

"But he could have driven around to the street behind Sweet Haven and parked there, then made his way to where my car was. The lot was almost full. I parked at the back in the last space."

"There are a lot of ice-cream lovers in Port Bliss." Sean closed his laptop and turned slightly toward her—only inches separated them. A blush tinted her cheeks pink. The dark brown—almost black—in her eyes transfixed him for a long moment.

Finally she slid her gaze away. "Sweet Haven also has sandwiches for the lunchtime crowd."

Until that moment, he hadn't realized he was holding his breath. He inhaled deeply and rose. "I'll keep you updated on what I find."

"What about the police officer outside? How long is he staying?"

"If you go somewhere, an officer will follow you while another one will remain at your house."

"What do I say to Sammy, who'll ask me a ton of questions about the officer being around?"

"That you're an important part of a case."

"What case?"

"A secret one? Kids love secrets."

"Do you have children?"

"No. I'm not married." He had been once, but that ended the day he walked in on his wife with another man. He'd wanted to try to work it out, but she didn't. They had gotten married too young, not even a full year after high school, where they had dated for their junior and senior years. She changed a lot, but so did he. He hadn't realized how much until that moment of finding her with a man in their house.

"Once I tell Sammy it's a secret, I'll never have any peace. He'll want to know every detail."

He towered over Aubrey, still sitting on the couch. "Then simply tell him…" Sean couldn't think of anything to say. "I have two nephews and one niece but haven't seen them as much as I used to when I lived in Amarillo. You'll figure something out."

"I'm glad you have so much confidence in me." Her gaze latched onto his.

And he couldn't look away. There was something about her that had kept him up a good part of last night viewing the courthouse surveillance tapes and the traffic cams all around the places she went yesterday. Then early this morning, he got up and called the owner of Sweet Haven Parlor about their video footage. The man agreed to meet Sean at his store. He was there before the owner arrived. It gave him an opportunity to look around the building and parking lot next to it.

Breaking eye contact, he stepped back, and in response to her last comment, he said, "Your reputation as a judge is excellent. Tough but fair."

"Some think those two words are opposites." She stood and smiled. "But thank you. Coming from a law enforcement officer, your words mean a lot to me."

The temperature in the room seemed to rise. He moved back another couple of feet and bumped into the chair across from the couch, then tipped his hat. "I'll keep you informed. 'Bye." He started for the office door.

"You forgot something."

His laptop. Heat burned his cheeks from embarrassment. He slowly rotated toward her and grabbed his computer. "Thanks."

When he left the house, he headed to the police officer sitting in his car in the driveway. "Officer Carter, call me if there's anything odd going on." He handed the younger man his business card. "And have the officer who replaces you do the same."

"Yes, sir. It's been quiet. The only things that have happened are Judge Madison's kids coming out here and you arriving."

"Let's hope it stays that way." Sean strode to his SUV and climbed into the driver's seat.

He drove to the police station, not far from the courthouse, to see the police chief, who usually worked Saturday mornings. Sean found him in his office and shook hands with him.

"Officer Carter says everything is quiet at the judge's house. What can I do for you?" Chief Juan Perez asked.

"I'd like your officers to be on the lookout for a white Chevy Malibu, most likely a recent model with a dent in its driver's-side back fender near the bumper. I have a partial Texas license plate number. The last three digits are two four nine. I'm heading to my office to run the information through the DMV, and I'll let you know what I find. I believe the driver was responsible for putting the dead rat and the judge's deceased husband's lost wedding ring in her car trunk yesterday."

"Sure, I'll let my police force know. Anything to help Judge Madison. I want the trial of Villa to go smoothly. Has anyone approached her about it?"

"No. I'm not sure this has anything to do with Bento Villa. A judge can sway a verdict in some cases, but there are other ways to change the outcome of a trial that are more effective. How are the people testifying against Villa doing?"

"Okay. The US Marshals are protecting the main person in an undisclosed place. In Villa's case, there's a lot of forensic evidence, as well as a video taken by a bystander." The police chief leaned forward and rested his elbows on his desk. "Could this have anything to do with her husband's murder?"

"Maybe, especially with returning the wedding ring. But why now, after two years have passed? I've been working on the case off and on since I came here, and not much new information has turned up."

"The crime didn't happen in my jurisdiction. I'm glad you're working it. Samuel was a good man."

"And the family should have closure." He of all people realized that, since there was no resolution to what had happened to his brother. Sean pushed to his feet. "Thanks again for the officer sitting outside the judge's house. I need to get to the courthouse before it shuts down for the weekend."

"Leave the information about the white car with my sergeant. He can run down the information you need and call you."

"Thanks." Sean left the police chief's office and stopped to give Sergeant Vic Daniels what he would need to run down the vehicle. Then Sean decided to walk to the courthouse across the street.

The day was perfect, with temperatures in the low seventies and a light breeze from the Gulf with smells he relished—fresh with a hint of brine. He circled the building before going inside, assessing its security before he went to the employee parking lot behind the courthouse. There were a handful of vehicles in that lot. He noted where Aubrey's car was yesterday and the locations of all the security cams. She obviously hadn't parked with the thought of making sure her car was in full view of the surveillance cameras. On Monday, that would need to change. As well, he would have a chat with the person who monitored the video feed. As he studied the best places where a deputy sheriff could be stationed near the rear exit, the sense of being watched rippled down his spine. He whirled and scanned the back of the building.

Someone had been at a window on the second floor looking outside but jumped back when he turned. It happened so fast, he couldn't even identify the person as a male or female. Aubrey's office was on that floor. He hurried into the courthouse and raced up the nearby stairs.

When he arrived in front of the entrance to Judge Madison's office, the door was ajar. Sean removed his gun and kicked the door wide-open, scanning the room as he moved forward. He turned slightly to the left and swept his gaze over a sitting area and a bookcase with every shelf filled, then onto the large desk with two chairs in front of it.

As he twisted toward the right, a large figure clad in

black lunged for him. The assailant raised his arm. In a split second, a hard object crashed into Sean's skull.

Aubrey slid the cookie sheet into the preheated oven, then straightened, her glance bouncing from the flour all over the counter to the vanilla spilled next to the sugar. Then she swung her attention to Sammy and Camy. The ingredients that went into making the cookies covered them from head to toe.

"Camy, you need to take off your shoes. You have an egg all over one of them. When did that happen?" Probably when she'd gone to answer her cell phone. She shouldn't have turned her back to answer it, though she'd hoped it was Sean with good news about the car. And it had been him, but with no updates concerning the white vehicle.

Her daughter glanced down and giggled. "Oops. Sorry. I wanted to crack one since Sammy did."

Her son puffed out his chest. "Mine didn't end up on the floor." He shook his head, sending more flour flying. "Who called earlier?"

"Texas Ranger McNair. As soon as Grandma gets back from church, I'm going down to the courthouse. A police officer is coming to pick me up." What had happened at the courthouse that Sean needed her there?

Sammy's eyes widened. "Can we go and use the siren?"

"No. This is business."

Camy's face scrunched up. "Business?"

The sound of the garage door going up indicated her mother was home. Aubrey hurried to clean up the mess while she said, "Go change and bring me your dirty clothes and, Camy, your tennis shoe with egg on it."

As she swiped a wet dishcloth over the floor where the egg had fallen, Aubrey realized this extra-messy kitchen was her fault in part because she hadn't kept her attention on her children as she usually did when they cooked together. She'd known better, but she'd promised to do something fun with them. She hadn't counted on Sean distracting her from afar. Then he called and said a police officer would be over to pick her up, and her full attention on her children vanished. He didn't say anything else, but the urgency in his voice indicated he hadn't told her everything. Something was wrong.

Her mother's chuckles coming from the entrance to the utility room pulled her focus from scooping up the last of the eggshells scattered everywhere. "Did a hurricane hit this kitchen while I was gone?"

"Yep. Hurricane Camy merged with Hurricane Sammy."

"I met Officer Adams as he pulled up to the house. He's here to pick you up. You might want to change your clothes while I finish taking care of this mess." Her mother's nose twitched. "What's burning?"

"Oh!" Aubrey shot to a standing position, grabbed the mitts and hurriedly took out of the oven the sheet full of slightly burned sugar cookies. "You know me and cooking."

"Go. I'll take care of this. Where are the kids?"

"Changing," Aubrey said as she headed out of the kitchen.

As the bell rang, her son barreled down the stairs, beating her to the front door and pulling it open. She knew Officer Cal Adams, her escort to the court-house. After asking the police officer to wait while she changed, Aubrey hastened to her bedroom and quickly threw on a pair of clean jeans and a T-shirt from the University of Texas. She made it back to the foyer within five minutes.

"Sammy, go in the kitchen and help your grandmother. Where's Camy? She wasn't in her room."

Sammy frowned and pointed toward the kitchen, then trudged down the hall.

Officer Adams grinned for a second before his expression became somber. "I think he's a bit disappointed I wouldn't let him go with us and turn on the siren. Tell Sammy we will another time. Texas Ranger McNair wanted you at the courthouse as soon as possible."

She walked beside Cal. "What's going on?"

"Someone was in your office."

"Who?"

"Don't know, but the person hit Texas Ranger McNair over the head."

"You should have told me right away. Was it bad? Did Sean get it looked at?"

Cal shook his head. "He isn't leaving your office, but he did clean it up. He says he's all right."

"Is he?"

"I predict he'll have a goose-egg knot on the side of his head, but I think he'll be okay. He didn't pass out totally."

"Totally?" Her heart began to race as she thought of one question after another: Who was in her office? Why? What were they after? But above all, was Sean really all right?

"Yeah, he was a little dizzy."

Her mother came into the entry hall. "What are your plans?"

"I'm going to my office for a while." Aubrey glanced past her mama to make sure Sammy and Camy weren't behind her listening. "Someone broke into it. I'm meeting Sean there."

"Does the break-in have to do with the trial?"

"Possibly."

"Please be careful, honey. I'll lock the door behind you and set the alarm. Then I need to get back to the kitchen. Sammy is holding the dustpan while Camy is sweeping the floor, which means she's rearranging where the flour is on the tile."

On the drive to the courthouse, Aubrey went over the events of the past twenty-four hours. When she arrived home yesterday, she'd been tired and concerned about the Villa trial. Now it was more than concern that pestered her. Was Samuel's murder tied to what was happening now? His wedding ring must mean it was—which raised the stakes of this trial even more.

Cal escorted her to her office on the second floor. A deputy sheriff who worked at the courthouse stood outside the door. When she entered, both of them stayed in the corridor while she looked at Sean sitting in a chair in front of her desk.

He glanced over his shoulder and attempted a smile that fell short. "Thanks for coming."

She walked to the other chair beside him and took a seat. "I heard you were hit, and from what I see it must be hurting. Can I get you a bag of ice or something else?"

"I took a couple of aspirin. Really, I'm fine. I've had worse. I'm just mad I couldn't catch him."

"You ran after him?"

"I tried, but by the time I stood and got my bearings, he was gone. I decided to stay. I didn't want to leave your office unprotected."

She surveyed the area. "It doesn't look like he took anything obvious. I'll need to go through my desk and files to make sure, though."

"If something was taken, it might help us determine what's going on here. I'll check the video feed later to see if I can tell how he got inside and possibly who he is, but that's a long shot. The brief glimpse I got was of a man with a ski mask on."

"I'll start with my desk. The computer is here, but I'll check to see if he got on it. I'll ask maintenance to change my lock immediately."

"I already have. One that will be harder to pick. The lock you have is an old one, and I think that's how he got in here. Who has a key to your office right now?"

"An assistant I share with Judge Rodriquez and Maintenance. You think it was one of them?"

"No, there were fresh scratch marks on the lock. But until I find out what's going on, you should have the only key. I did look at your file cabinets, and I didn't see any evidence he picked those locks, but you should still check everything in them. He risked breaking into your office for some reason. What was it?"

Aubrey made her way around to the other side of her desk and sat in her black stuffed chair. Sean started to rise, and she quickly said, "You stay there. I can do this. If I need you, I'll let you know." She opened the top left drawer and went through the personal items she kept in it. "After I've gone through my office, I'll drive your car and take you to the ER to make sure you're okay."

He opened his mouth to reply, but she held up her palm. "No arguments on that. If something is wrong and you didn't get help, it would be my fault." She shut the top drawer and reached for the bottom one.

Their gazes clashed. A war of emotions played across his face while Aubrey pulled the second compartment out.

A rattling sound sent shivers down her body as she stared at the coiled rattlesnake, poised to strike.

# FOUR

The sound of a rattlesnake shaking his tail reverberated through the office. Sean shoved to his feet while drawing his gun. Eyes wide, Aubrey leaped to her feet, thrusting her chair back at the same time the snake launched itself at her. Sean raised his weapon and shot the reptile. It fell to the floor as he rushed around the desk to Aubrey. The sudden movements sent the room tilting. He clutched the ledge of the desk and steadied himself.

The office door slammed open, and both guards aimed their guns into the room. Sean pivoted toward them. "I need a first-aid kit and something to take a dead rattlesnake to the hospital. I'm calling 911."

One deputy sheriff turned and left while the other stood inside the entrance. "Where was it?"

"In a desk drawer. This office will need to be thoroughly searched in case there's something else dangerous in here." Aubrey held her arm against her chest, the color washing from her face. Blood oozed from the bite wound on her forearm.

As he peered at the snake to make sure it was dead, Sean clasped her shoulders, guiding her back and sitting her down in her chair. "Hold your arm still and let it bleed." After calling 911 and requesting an ambulance, he said, "I want you to limit your movements. Help is on the way. I need to find a bag or container to take the snake to the hospital. That way they'll know exactly what bit you."

Aubrey stared at the rattlesnake. "First a rat and now a snake. Was this the purpose of the break-in?"

"Probably, but the crime might have been done for other reasons, too. Stay seated." Sean removed his tie and made a sling for Aubrey. "This will help keep your arm still." When he obtained a first-aid kit, he would place a sterile bandage over the wound. "I need to take off your rings on your left hand in case it swells."

She started to lift her arm toward him, but he stopped her. "The less movement you make, the less the venom will circulate through your body. I'll do it and keep them safe for you." Gently he removed her wedding and engagement rings and stuffed them in his pants pocket.

She looked up at him, sweat beading on her face. "Thanks."

"Let me know if your vision blurs or you become dizzy."

Aubrey attempted a smile, but it didn't last a second. "That's what I should be saying to you."

"The paramedics will be here soon."

"If I'm going to the hospital, you need to go, too."

"You don't need to worry about me."

"Sorry, I am."

The deputy sheriff who left to get the first-aid kit and paper bag hurried into the office and gave them to Sean. "I'm going downstairs to wait for the ambulance."

"I appreciate it."

As he left, Sean found a clean bandage and placed it over her wound, then he took the sack and placed the dead snake in it.

"After we're looked at, we need to come back here and see if the intruder took anything, especially concerning Villa's trial."

Sean plopped the bag onto the desk. "We?"

"I'm the only one who can tell you if something is missing or added. You can't do it without me."

"You'll have to stay in the hospital," he said as a bead of sweat rolled down her face.

"Maybe not. I hope I don't."

"My best friend was bit by a rattlesnake once. He was in the hospital for a few days."

"But my family needs—"

The door opening stopped her words. She glanced at the paramedics rolling a gurney into the office.

Sean leaned down and whispered into her ear, "I'll take care of your family. Don't worry about them. Focus on your recovery."

"Promise me you'll get your head wound checked out."

Her look of appeal made it impossible to say no. As the paramedics moved the desk to give them more room, Sean smiled and cupped her shoulder. "I will."

While the EMTs readied her to be transported to the hospital, Sean called the police officer on duty at her house, Officer Carter. After explaining what had happened, he said, "I want you to bring them to the hospital when she's admitted."

"The kids, too?"

Sean turned his back to Aubrey. "Leave that up to

Camilla Roberts. If the kids stay at the house, have the other officer stay and guard them. Let your police chief know, and have another officer at the house with her children. There's no doubt Judge Madison is being targeted. Someone wants to harm her."

Aubrey lay in her hospital bed, staring at the window with its blinds closed. The pain medication and muscle relaxer were starting to work. She prayed that the antivenin would, too, and quickly. She switched her attention to her left arm, which had a red streak moving up it. The nurse was marking how much it was spreading every hour.

She wished she knew more about rattlesnake bites. She wished she knew how Sean was doing. All she wanted to do was leave the hospital. She hated being here. The last couple days had made her think about Samuel and his murder. He'd left for work one morning, and she never saw him again.

Her eyelids grew heavy. She needed to stay awake. What if someone came in here and completed the job the rattlesnake had been planted in her office to do? But she couldn't keep her eyes open any longer. As she began to drift off, the sound of her door opening jerked Aubrey away from sleep.

She looked toward the entrance and didn't recognize the person entering. Instantly she fumbled for the call button. The man was dressed in blue scrubs with a name tag, but he hadn't been in her room before. After what had happened the last twenty-four hours, she couldn't shake her suspicions.

"I'm your nurse this evening. I wanted to check in

with you." He stopped next to her bed and peered at her left arm. "It looks like the red line is slowing down."

She didn't know what to say. Her heartbeat doubled its rate. Where was Sean?

"How are you feeling? Is the pain medication helping?" He moved even closer.

Words stuck in her throat. She kept replaying the rattlesnake attack while pressing the call button.

The door opened. The nurse swiveled his attention toward the entrance. "Judge Madison, I'm Deputy Sheriff Simpson. I've been assigned to guard you. I'll be right outside your door if you need me." He started to leave.

She'd seen him at the courthouse. He was a familiar face. "Wait!"

The deputy sheriff paused and glanced at her.

"I have a couple of questions."

Simpson approached her.

Aubrey stiffened and slanted a look at the nurse. "I'm fine. Thanks," she said in a dismissing voice.

He lifted his gaze to the deputy sheriff, then said, "If you need anything, push the call button."

The second he left, Aubrey relaxed, releasing a long sigh.

"Is something wrong, Judge Madison?" the deputy sheriff asked.

"After what happened at the courthouse, I'm anxious. Please make sure that whoever comes in here works here."

His forehead wrinkled. "Did that nurse give you any problems?"

"He was a stranger. That's the first time I saw him. Something didn't feel right."

"Ma'am, his outfit is similar to others on the floor, and he had a name tag."

"Deputy Simpson, after today I'm suspicious of everyone."

"I understand. I'll check into who he is."

"Thank you."

When the door closed behind the deputy sheriff, Aubrey lifted her shaky right hand and couldn't stop it from quivering.

Sean finally left the emergency room after being checked out. The test confirmed what he already knew—a concussion. He'd had one before and knew what it felt like. He was more concerned about Aubrey. A nurse told him she'd been taken to a room on the second floor. One reason he headed upstairs was to make sure the deputy sheriff assigned to guard her room was in place. But his main purpose was to see how Aubrey was doing. No one would tell him anything in the ER, even though they'd come into the hospital together.

Exiting the elevator, Sean immediately spied Deputy Simpson. Sean had requested him since he was one of the deputy sheriffs who worked at the courthouse. Aubrey would be familiar with him. While waiting to be treated, he'd talked with Police Chief Juan Perez and Sheriff Don Bailey to coordinate law enforcement officers guarding the judge during Bento Villa's trial. It was clear she was in danger, and the dead rat pointed to the Coastal Cartel. Later he would meet with his informant to see what he'd heard about the trial and the judge.

Sean stopped next to Simpson at the nurses' station down the hall from Aubrey's room. Why wasn't he at her door?

Simpson glanced at Sean then resumed his conversation with a nurse behind the counter. "Where is your nurse Chris Newton?"

"Chris called in sick today."

"Is there a problem?" Sean asked when he saw the surprised look on Simpson's face.

Keeping an eye on a room down the hall, Simpson answered, "He was with Judge Madison a few minutes ago in her room. At least his name tag said Chris Newton."

Sean started down the corridor, saying, "Get a picture of Newton and see if it was him or an impostor."

Simpson had left Aubrey unguarded in her room when he went to the nurses' station. When Sean had arrived, the deputy sheriff had his head turned away from her room while talking with the woman. Even if only for a couple of minutes, his action could have put her in jeopardy. Sean drew his gun, approaching 214 as though there was a crime in progress. He burst into her room, his gaze sweeping the area.

Aubrey's eyes grew round. "What's wrong?"

"Anyone in the bathroom?"

"No."

Sean moved to her bed, standing on the side that gave him a view of the whole room and the door. He told her about the nurse being out sick today. His hand on his weapon tightened. "Simpson is seeing if there's a photo of him to check if the person in here was Chris Newton."

Aubrey closed her eyes for a moment. "I knew something was wrong. That's why I asked Deputy Simpson to check on the nurse."

The red streak moving up her arm caught Sean's attention. "What did the doctor say?"

"I need to stay until they make sure the antivenin has taken care of the poison in my body. I want to go home, but the doctor says I'll probably be here for a couple of days. After what just happened, I don't want to stay."

"You'll have twenty-four-hour protection from now on. Someone will be outside your door."

"Someone I know, like Deputy Simpson?"

"Yes, and I'll be here some of the time." He would make sure Simpson and any guard understood the importance of not moving from the door.

"What about my mother and children?"

"I've taken care of that. Two people will be guarding them at all times."

"Thank you. I won't be intimidated by anyone behind this, but having my family protected makes me feel better." She stared at her left arm. "This cartel hasn't gone after many judges. Why now?"

"Bento Villa is one of Sanchez's lieutenants. Think of the information he knows on Sanchez and the Coastal Cartel."

"I know the government is trying to get him to testify against Sanchez."

Sean pulled a chair closer to the bed and sat.

"What did the doctor say about your head wound?" she asked.

"A mild concussion. The pain meds he gave me are helping the headache."

"You need to take it easy."

"I wish I could, but I promised you I'll do everything I can to find out what's going on."

"I need to see my children and Mama. I imagine they're worried."

"Officer Carter is bringing them up to the hospital. That way I can get him to drop me off at the courthouse to pick up my car."

"You shouldn't be on the highway tonight. Remember your concussion."

"That's why I've accepted your mother's invitation to stay at your house."

"Great!" Aubrey grinned. "My mama used to be a nurse before she came to live with me. I'll feel better if you have her nearby if you get dizzy, nauseated or whatever other symptoms you could have because of your concussion."

"And I'll feel better if I'm not thirty-five miles away if something else happens to you." His cell phone buzzed, and he slid it out of his pocket. "This is a text from Officer Carter. He just left your house. I need to let Simpson know they're coming and to meet them at the main entrance. I'll stay here."

Sean left the room, scanning the hallway before saying to the deputy sheriff, "Did you get a photo of Chris Newton?"

"Yes, the head nurse got one from the HR department, and it isn't the guy who was in the judge's room. No one saw a male nurse going into her room, but then, Judge Madison is down the hall from the nurses' station." Simpson passed the picture to Sean.

"That's why you can't leave this door."

"Yes, sir. I won't."

Sean looked down at the photo of a man in his early

thirties with dark hair and eyes and a slender build. "What did the guy look like? I want you as well as Aubrey to give a description to a sketch artist. I'll talk to the sheriff and make the arrangements, but right now I need you to go downstairs to the main entrance and wait for Officer Carter and Judge Madison's family. I'll be in the room with her while you're gone. After escorting them up here, go by the security office and see if there's any video footage of the fake Chris Newton. If there is, later I'll have you check the video since you saw him."

"Yes, sir."

As Sean watched the deputy sheriff walk to the elevator, he leaned back against the wall next to Aubrey's door. For a few seconds he focused on the constant throbbing at the back of his head. Was the man in her room earlier the person who'd attacked him and left the rattlesnake in Aubrey's office?

When Sean came back into Aubrey's hospital room, she knew something was wrong. She adjusted a pillow behind her for more support. "What's the bad news?"

"The guy who came into your room isn't the nurse Chris Newton. We have a photo of the real Chris Newton, and Simpson said it wasn't the same person. He's going to check hospital security footage for a picture of the fake nurse."

"That's not bad news. He's a lead to what's going on."

"I agree. Between you and Simpson, we'll get a good description, even if there isn't a good picture on the security footage."

"When will my kids and Mama be here?"

"Soon. Simpson will escort them up here." Sean stood at the sound of a light knock on the door and hurried to answer it. "Who is it?"

"It's me," Sammy said.

"Who is me?"

Giggles filled the air. "Sammy," he said in a louder voice.

"Camy."

Sean pulled the door open, and two four-year-olds rushed into the room, making a beeline for their mother.

Aubrey's mother rushed after them. "Stop!" When the two came to a halt, she made her way to them and put a hand on each one's shoulder. "Be careful, y'all. Remember your mama was bitten by a snake."

Camy wrinkled her nose. "O-ow. Sorry, Mama."

"Did ya keep it?" A hopeful wish laced Sammy's question.

"No, honey. He's gone."

"But I wanna look at it. I love snakes." Sammy stuck his lower lip out.

Aubrey patted the right side of the bed. "Y'all come over here and give me a hug."

"Gentle, Sammy and Camy." Her mother released her hold on them.

With her two children pressed against her right side, Aubrey mouthed the words *thank you* to her mama. For the next fifteen minutes, she enjoyed having Camy, Sammy and her mother with her. But she couldn't stop her yawn.

"Mama, when ya gonna be home?"

Aubrey kissed the top of Sammy's head, saying,

"Soon," and then did the same to Camy. "Now y'all do what your *abuela* tells you."

They both nodded.

While her mother grasped Sammy's and Camy's hands and moved toward the exit, Sean stepped closer to Aubrey, leaned down and whispered, "I'll be back after I get my car from the courthouse. Simpson will be outside your room until his replacement comes at midnight."

"Who's replacing Simpson?"

"One of the deputy sheriffs assigned to the courthouse."

"But you don't know who?"

"No. But I'll call the sheriff and find out." He took her hand. "I'm going to do everything I can to keep you safe and find out who is behind what's going on."

"Thanks." The exhaustion she'd been fighting ever since the fake nurse came into her room swirled about her, demanding she close her eyes. Yet she fought it, trying to keep her eyes open as Sean released her hand and crossed to the door, dimming the lights right before leaving. No matter how much she tried to stay awake, she couldn't. Darkness swooped in to engulf her.

Some time later Aubrey shifted in the bed, trying to roll over on her left side. Pain shot up her arm, and her eyelids flew open. For a few seconds in the low light, she couldn't figure out where she was. She struggled to sit up. A woman dressed in scrubs stood next to her bed.

Disoriented, Aubrey gasped.

"I'm Fay Patterson, the nurse on the night shift assigned to you. I need to check your arm."

After what happened earlier with the fake nurse, Aubrey hesitated, searching for the call button.

"Aubrey, she works for the hospital. She came on duty at eleven."

The sound of Sean's voice shifted her attention to a darkened area of the room. He sat in a lounge chair. "How long have you been back? What time is it?"

"I've been here for hours. It's one in the morning."

She couldn't believe she'd been asleep for five hours. It felt like she'd just closed her eyes a few minutes ago.

After the nurse examined her arm and took her blood pressure, she left the room. Aubrey caught a glimpse of the deputy sheriff on duty and relaxed.

"I'm glad to see Bill Lockhart here. He often makes sure I get to my car safely at the end of the day. I feel better when I know the guard."

Sean rose and came to the bed, taking his seat next to her from earlier. "And I'm glad to see you're getting some sleep."

"How about you? I thought you were going to stay with my mama and my kids."

"I ended up relieving Simpson so he could go downstairs and search for the fake nurse on the security tapes. He returned at eleven, and I hated to go to your house that late, but I made sure there are sufficient officers guarding your family."

She was discovering that Texas Ranger Sean McNair covered all angles of a situation. That comforted her. Despite what had happened to her earlier, she felt safe with him by her side. "Did he get a picture of the guy on the footage?"

"Yes. He tracked the impostor when he left this room first, but the guy was good. He never showed his face on the camera. We got a glimpse of the black pickup he drove out of the parking lot but not its license plate number. Then Simpson went to the time the man came into your room and tracked him back to when he came into the hospital. Still no sight of his face. Tomorrow I'll have the police see if they can trace the truck after it left the parking lot, capture its license plate number on a traffic cam and possibly even determine where it went. Although the last is a long shot, since there aren't that many cameras here as in a bigger city."

"Anything on the real Chris Newton?"

Sean shook his head. "The police chief notified me that Newton's apartment was empty. No sign of a break-in. But the man's car is missing. It wasn't in the building's parking lot."

"No one knows where he is?"

"I'm afraid not. The police are looking for the real Chris and his car."

"That doesn't sound good for Chris Newton."

"The police are treating this as a missing-person case with possible foul play."

Aubrey raked her fingers through her short hair, frustrated she was confined to a hospital room. She glanced at her left arm and noticed that the red streak hadn't spread much since she went to sleep. A good sign. Maybe she would be able to leave here later today.

"Simpson will work with a sketch artist first, then you can. Hopefully that will give us a good picture of what he looks like. Then we'll run it through the database to see if we can come up with a name for the fake nurse."

"I'll help any way I can." She looked at his face,

noting the lines of exhaustion, and added, "Have you got any sleep lately?"

He smiled. "Actually, a couple of hours. That lounge chair isn't too uncomfortable."

"You might not have been required to stay in the hospital, but you need rest. You were hurt, too."

Sean stood. "I'm going to. There's a lot to do in the morning."

His cell phone buzzed. He pulled it out of his pocket and looked at the screen. A frown spread over his face as he started for the door.

"What's wrong?"

Sean stopped and twisted around to face her. She couldn't see his expression well because of the shadows, but his tense stance screeched that whatever his text said wasn't good. "Chris Newton's body has been found."

# FIVE

Late the next afternoon, Sean pulled into the driveway at Aubrey's house and switched off the engine, then turned toward her in the front passenger seat. "I think you should have stayed in the hospital another night."

"Remember, my mother was a nurse. She talked with the doctor, and if there's a problem, I'll return to the hospital. I'm canceling court tomorrow. I'll be seeing Dr. Rains in the morning. I'll be able to rest more at home. I feel safer—especially with you here." Aubrey's gaze locked with his. "You saved my life yesterday. When I saw that rattlesnake, at first I couldn't even move. If I'd thought to slam the drawer closed the second I saw the snake, I wouldn't have been bitten. I most likely would have been bitten a second time if you hadn't taken care of it. One of the reasons I think I got to come home earlier was your quick thinking and knowledge of what to do if you get bitten."

"I'm trying to figure out why someone is going after you. If they wanted to delay the trial, it would only be for a few days. So what's his objective?"

"The primary witness is being protected. What if he thought an extra day or so would help Villa's minions locate the witness? A person's life doesn't mean much to some people."

"That's what I was thinking." Sean put his hand on the door lever. "Are you ready to be mobbed by two kids?"

She chuckled. "Yes. They're the reason I wanted to come home. I don't want them worrying about me."

"Before we go inside, I need to give you back your rings, since your fingers aren't swollen anymore." Sean withdrew them from his pocket and gave them to Aubrey.

She stared at the rings in the palm of her hand and closed her fingers around them. "Thanks." She tucked it away in her sweater's pocket and climbed from the car.

As Sean exited the SUV, the front door swung open to Sammy trying to leave. Officer Carter stood near the entrance on the porch and prevented Aubrey's son from stepping outside. Sean walked beside her and supported her as she mounted the stairs. The police officer moved to the side and opened the screen door.

Sean slowed Sammy's charge toward his mother. "Whoa, young man."

Sammy slowed for a few seconds, but when he threw his arms around Aubrey, she rocked back on her heels. At a more sedate pace, Camy also approached and hugged her mama.

"Y'all, let's go inside."

Sammy planted himself on Aubrey's right side while Camy was on her left. Sean led the way into the house, where Camilla stood waiting for them.

"I'm glad you're home." She kissed Aubrey's cheek. "We've been praying for you."

Sammy straightened his shoulders. "Mama, I asked God to get the bad guy."

"I did, too," Camy added.

With her right arm, Aubrey brought her twins to her. "We're safe."

"Is your arm broken?" Camy pointed at Aubrey's sling that held her left arm.

"No. Keeping it like this helps protect it. I need to be careful. It's sore right now."

"Okay, you two. You have a mess to pick up in the den." Camilla corralled the twins and steered them toward the back of the house.

While Aubrey headed into the living room, Sean made sure the front door was locked, then followed. "You look a little pale. Are you okay?"

She eased down on the couch. "Yes. Just tired—and overwhelmed."

"Overwhelmed?"

"I forget how my children are so enthusiastic about everything they do, especially Sammy." She sighed and reclined against the back cushion, her eyes closing.

Maybe coming home early wasn't a good idea. All day she'd tried to downplay what had happened to her and the toll it had taken on her body.

As he sat at the other end of the couch, she rolled her head to the side and looked right at him. "When is Sheriff Bailey going to come see you?"

"Soon. Another body was found near Newton's by the cadaver dog. It had been dead for months. He's also bringing the sketch artist who's been working with Simpson on the description of the suspect in your room yesterday. He wants your input."

"I'm not going to forget that man's face, especially

his eyes. Dark. Intense. Thinking about him gives me the shivers." She crossed her arms and hugged them to her chest. "I want us to meet in my office. It's more private." She lowered her voice. "I don't want the kids to know about the guy in my hospital room. In fact, I wish we could sneak the sheriff inside, especially if he's wearing his uniform."

"Do you want him to wear regular clothes?"

She shook her head. "I don't think there's any way I can shield my twins from what's happening."

"And Sammy wants to know every juicy detail?"

"Right. Maybe I can get Mama to take them outside in the backyard when he arrives. Let them run around and tire themselves out. We have a six-foot privacy fence. The deputy could be on the patio to watch over them. There's a lock on the gate. If I can keep their life as normal as possible, Sammy will eventually get bored and move on to something else."

"I know he's only four, but does he like any sports?"

"Soccer. Even Camy likes it. Sammy saw a photo of his dad in his soccer uniform when he was in school. He wants to do everything his father did."

"Then you have a soccer ball?"

She nodded. "He keeps it in his room."

"I can knock the ball around with both of them, so they don't think of me as a law enforcement officer all the time. That might help take their mind off what's happening."

Her smile lit her face. "That would be great, especially tomorrow when I'm home. I'll get a ton of questions from Sammy about why I'm not going to work."

Sean texted the sheriff, who replied that he was ten

minutes away. "He'll be here soon. I'll let your mother and Officer Carter know what we're going to do."

As he rose, Aubrey did, too. "I'm going into my office."

He made his way to the den. While Sammy played with his superheroes and Camy colored, Sean motioned to Camilla to come talk to him across the room. He didn't want the twins to overhear.

Camilla approached him and whispered, "Everything okay?"

"Yes." Sean kept his attention on the twins and murmured, "The sheriff is coming to see us. He's bringing a sketch artist to get a picture of the guy yesterday in Aubrey's room. Officer Carter will go out back with you and the kids. Aubrey doesn't want them to know about the sheriff. I'll come out later to kick a soccer ball around with them."

"Good idea. Until about five minutes ago, I've been fielding one question after another from Sammy. I'll take them outside before the sheriff arrives."

"Thanks. We'll be in Aubrey's office. I'll bring the soccer ball when I come out."

Camilla turned to her two grandchildren with a big grin on her face. "Remember your mama has to rest and take it easy. I'm tired of being inside the house. Let's go outside and play."

Sammy pumped his arm into the air while Camy clapped. They both jumped up and quickly closed the space between them and their grandmother.

Sammy stopped next to Sean and tilted his head back, his big hazel eyes fixed on him. "Can you come, too?"

"I'll be outside in a little while. In the meantime, I'll send Officer Carter out back."

"Yes!" Sammy grinned from ear to ear.

As Camilla and the kids left, Sean headed toward Aubrey's office. He heard the back door closing ten seconds before someone knocked on the front one. Sean hurried to answer it and let Sheriff Don Bailey into the house. Officer Carter followed behind him.

"The kids just went out back with Mrs. Roberts. When I relieve you in a while, you should return to the front porch."

Officer Carter nodded and walked toward the rear of the house.

"Aubrey is in her office. She doesn't want her children to know what's going on."

"I understand. I have an inquisitive grandson." The sheriff gestured toward the woman who accompanied him. "This is Maria Cortez, the sketch artist."

Sean shook the middle-aged woman's hand. "Nice to meet you."

She opened her pad and tore off the top sheet. "This is what Officer Simpson thinks the man looks like. I don't want to show the judge the picture until after she gives me her information."

"Thanks." Sean studied the drawing. The hair on the impostor looked just like the hair on Chris Newton's photo in the hospital database. Dark, almost black, medium-length strands, with bangs pulled to the left. He wore the glasses from Newton's picture. The only thing that didn't fit was the brown eyes. The color was too dark, and there was something else he couldn't put his finger on about the eyes. Aubrey had called them intense, and they were, but he couldn't say that about Newton's.

"While she's working with the judge, I thought we could go over what we have so far. We can use the living room. Everyone else is out back." Sean gestured across the hall. "I'll take Ms. Cortez to Aubrey."

When they entered the office, Aubrey's eyes opened, and she sat up straight on the small couch. After he introduced the sketch artist, he left them to talk and crossed to the living room. Sean took his seat across from the sheriff in the lounge chair and withdrew a pad and pen.

"The cadaver dog that found Newton's body in the vicinity of where his car was found discovered another body, and then an additional two others. We're processing the area and hoping there are no more."

"So the murderer used the same place to dispose of the people he killed?"

"That's what it appears to be. So far there are four."

Sean curled his hand into a fist. "Any idea who the other three are?"

"One was a known member of the Coastal Cartel. The other two bodies are decomposed beyond visual identification. It will take more time to figure out who they are. No IDs were on any of the victims."

This all came back to the cartel. "Are the prosecutors on this case being protected? If the cartel is coming after the judge, they might also target the government attorneys."

The sheriff nodded. "Each has a bodyguard."

Sean rose. "I'll be right back."

When he entered the kitchen, he made a beeline for the large window that overlooked the backyard to check on Sammy and Camy. The two were running around, laughing and chasing each other. The sight of them was heartwarming.

At one time he'd wanted a family, but his job often got in the way. When he became a Texas Ranger, he realized he would devote his whole life to his job—and yet he felt he was missing out on something.

Sean returned to the living room. "How did you find Newton's car?"

"We tapped into its GPS navigation system to find its location. I guess the killer didn't care if Newton was found. I wonder if he was trying to make a statement. Can we keep the information about the other bodies quiet for now? The guy might be trying to intimidate someone."

"Or doesn't care if they're discovered. That's why I'm hoping we can figure out who was in the judge's hospital room." Sean's head throbbed. The pain was less intense than it had been, but he still had a reminder that someone had hit him over the head recently. He kneaded the tight muscles at the back of his neck. "Please send me all the crime-scene photos. Right now, my priority is to protect the judge, but when she's in the courtroom, I'll be able to follow some leads."

"One of the leads we found this morning was a black wig and blue scrubs in a dumpster not far from the hospital. They were sent to the lab to find if there are any clues about who wore them. There may be DNA from his real hair under the wig."

"I hope so."

"We'll put out the sketch from Officer Simpson and

Judge Madison. Maybe someone will recognize the guy."

"He knew what he was doing. Not one camera caught his face. A pro." Sean pushed to his feet. "I'd like a copy of the autopsy reports of Newton and everyone found nearby."

The sheriff stood and left the living room with Sean. "I'll keep you informed as the case develops."

"Same here. The next couple of weeks will be tense." Sean needed to talk to his informant to see if he'd heard any rumblings. He hoped he could find him. Something else was going down that went beyond Villa's murder trial.

As Sean opened the office door, a soft laugh echoed through the room. When he spied Aubrey relaxed next to the sketch artist on the couch, the sound of her laughter eased his tension. He loved hearing it. For a few seconds, he relished it.

Aubrey glanced up. "I think we have a good composite that will help you find him."

The sketch artist held up the drawing. "I did one first without her seeing Officer Simpson's version. When I compared the two, there were little differences between them. I called the police chief. The officer is on his way here. Once we reconcile the two pictures, I'll have a drawing for you to use."

"That's good to hear." Sean hung back at the door while the sheriff sat in a chair near Aubrey. "I'm going out back. Officer Carter will return to the front porch."

Aubrey looked at him. "I'll let you know when everyone leaves."

As he left the office, Sean couldn't shake the weariness and apprehension he saw in her face. She needed to rest without worrying about what was happening in Port Bliss, but that would be difficult with her being in the middle of all that was going on.

He strolled toward the back door. One thing nagged him about what had occurred these past few days. The rat was a trademark of the Coastal Cartel. But why the rattlesnake in her desk drawer? It didn't fit what he knew about them.

Something didn't feel right to him.

Monday evening Aubrey shut her laptop and put it on the coffee table, throwing the living room into darkness. She closed her tired eyes, eager to get to court tomorrow. All she wanted was this trial to be over and her life to return to normal. But would it ever be normal again?

Ever since her husband was murdered, her life had consisted of making it through one day at a time. She'd never felt her job was dangerous like Samuel's, but now she'd discovered it could be. Although she loved the law and her work, after this trial she needed to reconsider what she should do, especially because of her children.

Was that why she hadn't put her wedding and engagement rings on after Sean returned them? Instead they were upstairs in her jewelry box. All she knew at the moment was that she was confused. She was tired of feeling like her life was in limbo. For her children's—and her own—sake, she needed to look forward. She prayed her husband's murder could be solved so she could put the past behind her.

"What are you doing sitting in the dark?" Sean paused in the entrance from the dimly lit entry hall.

She gasped and reached over to the end table to switch on the lamp. "I like the dark. I often sit in the darkness and think about the day."

Sean smiled. "I just wanted to make sure you're all right." He covered the distance to her, turned off the light and sat next to her.

With their arms touching, she could feel the tension leave her body. "Thanks for hitting the soccer ball around. Sammy didn't want to stop talking about it and go to bed. Even Camy had fun. They needed that break and the exercise."

"I hope to do it again. I had fun with them."

She hoped he could, too. She wondered why he didn't have children. He would make a good father. Her kids' giggles had filled the air the whole time he was playing with them. She loved that sound.

"What were you thinking about earlier in the dark?"

"The case. My future."

He covered her hand on the couch between them. "Anything you want to share?"

"I checked the news sites online and saw the composite picture of the impostor has been released. I hope the police get tips on his whereabouts." She turned toward Sean. Although she couldn't make out his features very well in the dark, she imagined his expression—confident, caring and committed. As though compelled by an invisible force, she reached out with her free hand to cup his face. "I also thought about my job. I can't put my family in danger. I've been a judge for five years here, some of it before my twins were born, and never felt fear for my life or my family's."

"This is when we have to trust God and put our lives in His hands. A person crossing a street can be hit by a car or by lightning. We have to live each day to the fullest, take precautions where we can, but not worry about things that may or may not happen. It's exhausting and takes away from the moment you're living in."

"It's hard to lose someone close to you, especially unexpectedly. That morning, the day my husband was murdered, I said goodbye to him, never considering I wouldn't see him again alive. In fact, we were arguing over him having to work on a day we'd planned to go to Padre Island. The last thing he said to me was he would make it up to me, then he kissed me on the cheek and hopped into his SUV. I didn't even watch him leave because Camy started crying. I had to run back into the house. If only I'd known that was the last time…" Her throat closed. She'd relived that morning many times, but she'd never been able to voice how it would have made a difference if she'd known it was the last time she would see him alive.

"I regretted the things I said to my younger brother when he left Amarillo to come down here," Sean said. "He was nineteen, reckless and impulsive. He wanted to work on an oil rig, and he loved the water. He hated where we lived. We'd talk over the phone occasionally, but usually we missed each other. When my brother went missing, I felt like I'd let him and my father down. Dad had wanted me to watch out for Jack. I've searched for the past two years and can't find anything about what happened to my little brother."

"Sometimes not knowing what happened is worse than knowing. You don't have any resolution about your brother."

Sean drew Aubrey against his side. "I've tried to solve both of their cases, but I keep running into dead ends. Their cases may forever remain unsolved, although I think both are connected to the Coastal Cartel in some way."

She shuddered against him when she thought about what the cartel had done to her husband. She'd thought she'd dealt with Samuel's death, but this trial was renewing the memories she'd tried to keep buried. "My office used to be Samuel's. When I was elected to be a judge again, I turned it into my workspace at home. At first, it was hard to be in that room, but now there's very little of Samuel in the office."

"I know you let me go through his stuff after his death and take what I needed to work on his case. Have you found anything since then?"

"Not since that last time a year ago. If I had, I'd have given it to you. I want his killer to be found and prosecuted. Then I'll know he won't be able to murder anyone else."

Sean relaxed against her. "I see what you mean about sitting in the dark. It's more calming when discussing a difficult subject. I may have to try it."

She chuckled. "I'm glad to help."

"Are you going to follow the doctor's orders about work?"

"Yes, only a half day tomorrow. We'll have opening remarks. But on Wednesday, I plan to do a full day. The quicker this trial is, the faster my family will be safe again." She yawned, the long day catching up with her.

"It sounds like you're tired."

"I am. Two children will do that to a parent."

Sean rose and held his hand out to help Aubrey up. "I need a pillow and a blanket."

"Where are you sleeping?"

"Here, on the couch. I already talked with your mother. She said she could share your bedroom, but I want to be downstairs, near the staircase and front entrance."

"I have to admit I feel better having you here." Aubrey flipped on the overhead light as she left the living room. "I'll get what you need and help you make up a bed on the couch."

She started up the stairs, but Sean stopped her. "You need your rest. I don't need much. I'm a light sleeper and can fall asleep just about anywhere."

Aubrey glanced over her shoulder and continued upstairs. "I wish I could do that. One of the reasons I hated the hospital was I couldn't get much rest there."

Sean followed her down the second-floor hallway to her linen closet at the end. After she gave him a light blanket and a pillow, their hands briefly making contact, he strolled toward the staircase. "Sleep well," he said then disappeared from view.

She left the walk-in linen closet, her hands tingling from touching his. Talking to him was so easy and comfortable. She rarely shared her thoughts about Samuel and his death, even with her mother. But the words tumbled from her as though she and Sean had been friends for years.

If she'd been in her office alone when she opened that drawer, she could have died because the sight of the rattlesnake paralyzed her. He'd saved her life. That act had forged a bond between them that she'd never had with another—even Samuel.

After Sean escorted Aubrey to her office and checked the area, he left with two deputy sheriffs guarding her.

He was going to meet his informant, a man who lived on the street. Most people didn't really see him. He had a talent of being almost invisible with others. And he was a good listener, hearing bits and pieces of information that often helped Sean with his cases.

He went to a coffee shop near the marina and bought a cup and two bear claws, Nate's favorite pastry. After parking, Sean walked along the shore to the place he was supposed to meet Nate. He sat on the trunk of a downed tree and placed the coffee and pastries for Nate on the ground behind him. His informant would have it after he left. As he turned back around to face the sea, he glimpsed Nate in the midst of the tall grass along the shore.

"Have you heard anything about who was going after Judge Madison?"

"One of the top cleaners for the Coastal Cartel is in the area. It's made a few people anxious, especially members of the cartel around here. I've heard rumors recently flying around that there's an internal battle on who controls the group."

"Against Sanchez?"

"Yep, although that's just speculation because of the cleaner."

That could mean an all-out war with more victims. "Is the cleaner the person who left a snake in her office?"

Nate chuckled. "No way. From what I've heard about this guy, he's direct and wants to do the job himself. He doesn't sound like a person who would leave a rattlesnake."

"Have you heard anything about the burial ground that was found?"

"Who hasn't? That's all people have been talking about for the past couple of days."

"If you hear anything about Judge Madison or a possible war within the cartel or with another cartel, call me. I have a burner phone you can use."

"Leave it by the food. I'll only use it if there's an emergency. Cell phones can be hacked."

Sean walked away, hoping there wasn't a war between factions in the cartel. He'd heard last month that Sanchez was ill. Was that the reason for an attempted coup? Where did Villa fit in on what was going down? And how did the cleaner fit into all of this?

When Sean returned to his SUV, he headed toward where the bodies had been found. He'd heard from the sheriff there was another one discovered late last night, not where the others were clustered but nearby, so they were increasing their search perimeter.

Twenty minutes later, Sean arrived at the place, the area roped off. He would be assisting in finding the identities of the ones who hadn't been ID'd yet. Since he'd arrived in Port Bliss two years ago, he'd always been involved in trying to figure out the names of missing people found and if there was a connection to Jack. There was always the possibility one of the bodies could be his brother. He'd examined the photos sent to him from this burial ground, but for the older corpses, the photos told him little. He would visit the ME processing the bodies.

Sean covered the short distance to Sheriff Don Bailey and shook his hand. "Hopefully this will give some families closure on their missing person."

"I hope so. Another body was just discovered near

the one from last night. They're working on uncovering him. From what I've seen of the legs, the person was in the ground long enough to be almost fully decomposed, the same as the one nearby. It's been transported to the morgue." The sheriff started walking north.

"I'll go there when I leave here."

Don pointed to each hole as they wove their way through the burial ground. "We actually identified another body this morning from the missing-person list—Miguel Cruz. That makes four so far. He hadn't been buried long. Those are the easier ones."

"Did he work for the cartel?"

The sheriff slowed his pace. "As a matter of fact, he was a low-level smuggler."

"Any clues from the items that the fake nurse threw away in the garage bin?"

"Not one piece of hair other than from the wig."

Sean had wished for something to help ID the killer. "He might be bald. That could account for no hair left behind. Maybe we should release a composite of the guy as bald."

"It won't hurt, and might help us."

"If this was the work of a cleaner I've heard is in the area, it might not make much difference, but we have to try."

The sheriff scowled. "A cleaner? I hadn't heard that. Who told you?"

"A reliable source. I'll be letting Chief Perez know, too. The deaths may start skyrocketing."

Sean watched a team uncovering the most recent body. He stepped over to the hole and looked down. The skeleton of a mostly decomposed body lay in the dirt, but what grabbed Sean's full attention was a ring on a bony finger.

A ring that had belonged to his brother—a ring of their dad's that Sean had given Jack.

# SIX

When Aubrey had dismissed everyone in the Villa trial for the day, she quickly left the courtroom, making her way to her chambers to meet Sean. She was glad she was only going to be here for half a day. She hadn't slept very well last night. She kept going over her talk with Sean. In the middle of all that was happening, his presence made her feel safe. Although they weren't going through the exact same situation, they were both mourning a lost loved one and lacked information about what had happened to them.

With a deputy sheriff accompanying her, she opened the door to her office that was connected to the courtroom. When she saw Sean across from her, she smiled, her heart increasing its beat at the sight of him, dressed in his long-sleeved white shirt, tan pants, brown boots and off-white cowboy hat, with his Texas Ranger star pinned over his heart. But when she looked into his Caribbean-blue eyes, she knew something was wrong.

She waited until the deputy sheriff crossed to the exit and left the office before she asked what was up.

"I found my younger brother today at the burial ground the police found. They discovered his grave this morning."

"I'm so sorry. Are you sure it was him? He disappeared two years ago. He would have been in the ground possibly that long."

"Yeah, I know. A body decomposes faster in a warm climate. Two things indicate it was Jack—the unique ring on his finger and a break of his left arm just under the elbow. The ME will get his records from the Amarillo hospital to compare the break, but when I saw it and the ring, I knew it was Jack."

She walked to him and hugged him. "Are you all right?"

"Yes—no." Pulling back, he sighed. "I mean, I knew in my gut he was dead, but I guess I didn't realize there was always a small part of me hoping he was alive and that one day I would find him."

"Keeping hope is what humans do." Aubrey shrugged out of the black robe and laid it over a chair nearby. "You said my husband started investigating what happened to him after he went missing. It should have been the local police, so why did he begin working on a missing-person case?"

"Was there a connection with your husband? Was he an informant? Law enforcement officers use informants all the time. I've wondered if Jack was one for Samuel, but I don't know for sure. Your husband started looking into his case and was killed three days later. A coincidence or a connection? That was one of only two cases he was working on. I've gone over and over Samuel's paperwork and can't find a tie. All our boss knew was that he was following a lead on the Coastal Cartel. That's what he told the major the day before."

"As you know, I've given you everything in Samuel's office."

"Could he have put something from a case somewhere else?"

"He kept his work separate from his personal life." Samuel had always kept his job private from her, even though she was a judge and had seen all kinds of horrific crimes in her job. She'd wished he would share with her the hardships that she saw leaving a mark on him. "He wouldn't talk about his cases outside of that office, and even in there, he didn't share much. I didn't know what he investigated, although I suspected he was looking into the cartel. Samuel's younger brother nearly died from taking too many opiates after a motorcycle accident."

"Jack had a friend who died from an overdose, too. I was always worried Jack would follow Ted. They had been close. After Ted's death, Jack left Amarillo."

"And you couldn't protect him anymore?"

Sean nodded.

"You said you were meeting with your informant this morning. Did he have any clues to help us figure out what's going on?"

"Us?"

She put her balled hands on her waist. "You may be leading the case, but I'm an officer of the court. The integrity of the trial before me is at stake."

"My informant thinks a war between factions in the Coastal Cartel is brewing."

She closed her eyes and released a long breath. "Should we increase security at the courthouse even more?"

"I already told the sheriff this morning to put more security on Villa. I think Villa's definitely involved in some way."

"There's a lot of money and power at play. I want to make sure the trial is a safe haven for witnesses and everyone involved." Aubrey stepped over to her desk and stared at the bottom drawer, where the rattlesnake had been. She reached out to open it to get her purse, but her hand shook as she unlocked the drawer, then stopped a few inches from the handle. Earlier this morning, Sean had put it in that drawer. She wanted to get over her nervousness and open it herself now, but she didn't think she could.

Sean bent around her and grasped it, then tugged it open. He pulled out her pocketbook, closed the door and locked it again.

Aubrey instinctively moved back. "Even with the lock on the drawer, I'm going to have to find another place to put my purse. I thought I could do it. And in time I will, but not with all that's going on right now."

"It's always good to be cautious. Are you hungry? We can grab something from a drive-through for a late lunch."

"Sounds good. I have a feeling Sammy and Camy will want all my attention when I get home."

"A hamburger?" Sean walked with her to the door and opened it.

"Yes."

Sean made a call to the security office in the court-house as they walked down the stairs to the first floor. "We're leaving for the day. Any problems?"

When he hung up, she asked, "Everything okay?"

"Yes, all's clear. There's a deputy sheriff stationed in the parking lot with a bomb-sniffing dog, as well as the usual one at the rear building door."

"You think that's where the rat was put in my car?"

"No, the video footage of that day says otherwise. But there are ways to get around security cameras, so to be on the safe side, a deputy is patrolling the parking lot."

"You're thinking there could be a car bomb planted?"

"It's one of the tools that the Coastal Cartel uses."

Aubrey shivered at the thought of a bomb going off. Her step hesitated as she neared the hallway leading outside.

Sean stopped and faced her. "I've been studying and learning everything I can about the cartel. If I have anything to do with it, you'll be okay."

Aubrey looked into the kindness of his eyes and knew she was in good hands. Not only Sean's, but the Lord's. She had to trust Him, or she would fall apart and want to hide from life. "Thanks."

At the exit, Deputy Sheriff Lockhart stood guard, grinning. "It's so good to see you back at the courthouse."

"I appreciate you being one of my guards at the hospital."

"I'm not gonna let that killer come after you," the deputy said vehemently while he held the door open.

"Thanks, Bill. See you tomorrow."

As Aubrey headed out into the spring afternoon, she scanned the area around her as though a sniper was lying in wait to shoot her. "I can't wait to get home and take off this bulletproof vest immediately after I greet my kids."

"I've grown used to wearing one when necessary. It's saved my life a couple of times."

"I know the reason behind having one on, but sitting

in my chair in the courtroom wearing it makes me sad for what's going on in our society."

Sean unlocked his SUV and opened the door on the passenger side. "I confront that every day, which only makes my job more important. Someone has to protect the people who can't protect themselves. I hope to find justice for your husband and my brother, but also others who have been hurt."

His words reassuring her, Aubrey relaxed against the front seat. For a moment she let the exhaustion drain from her body, until she realized Sean sounded so much like Samuel. And her husband had died for his beliefs.

While Aubrey took a nap, Sean played in the backyard with Sammy and Camy. Hopefully the kids' loud laughter wouldn't bother her. The sound of merriment in the midst of what was going on made him hopeful he would find the people behind Samuel's and Jack's murders.

Sean moved with the soccer ball toward the makeshift goal area at the rear of the property. He passed it to Camy, who kicked at it, missing. Her second attempt sent the ball a few feet closer to the goal. Sammy danced around, trying to stop anyone from scoring. Again, Sean set Camy up, and this time she slammed the ball toward the bedsheet hanging as the backdrop. Sammy threw himself at the ball and missed.

Camy jumped up and down, pumping her fist into the air. "I did it!" She ran toward Sean and threw her arms around his legs, the biggest smile on her face.

Frowning, Sammy approached his sister. "I'm still ahead," he said and stuck his tongue out.

Sean ignored Sammy's behavior and instead picked up Camy and swung her around. "I knew you could do it." He hadn't thought it possible that she could grin any bigger, but she did. "I don't know about you two, but I'm ready to sit and rest. You've worn this guy—" he tapped his fingers against his chest "—out. I think your *abuela* has brought out some lemonade and cookies. I'm starving."

Sammy stuck out his chest. "I helped her this morning making 'em."

As Sean set Camy on the ground, she said, "I did, too. I didn't make a mess crackin' the egg." She glared at her twin.

"It's a girl's job anyway." Sammy started for the patio.

"I think everyone needs to learn to cook. I've made my share of food, and I want it to taste good, so I learned to cook."

Sammy stopped. "You did?"

"Sure. I live alone. I'm the only one who cooks for me at my home."

The little boy's eyes widened. He straightened his shoulders. "My *abuela* is teachin' me."

"Me, too." Camy tramped to the food and snatched up a cookie. After stuffing one into her mouth, she picked up a lemonade to wash down the dessert.

Then Sammy followed suit, but instead of one cookie he shoved two in and gave Camy a triumphant look.

She stomped her foot and turned her back on Sammy. "You mean!"

Okay. He should set boundaries, right? "Sammy, you need to tell your sister you're sorry. Eating cookies isn't a competition." Sean sat in the chair near the table with the refreshments. He took a cookie and bit off a small part, chewing slowly. "Mmm. Now that's the way to enjoy a cookie. These are great. Both of you did a great job making them. Too bad you didn't get to really enjoy the cookies because you almost inhaled them." He picked up the last one while Sammy watched. Camy's back was still to both of them. Sean stood and went to the little girl. "This is yours. They're delicious."

With her eyes glistening, she grabbed the cookie and slowly ate it. "Thanks."

Sammy came to his sister's side. "Sorry."

Sean clasped the boy's shoulder then Camy's. "Family is important. Family needs to stick together. Love each other."

Sammy nodded. Then Camy did.

"Good. Let's go in and see if we can get one more cookie each. That ought to hold us until dinner." Sean glanced toward the back door.

Aubrey stood in the entrance. The sight of her surprised him. Usually he was always aware of his surroundings, but he hadn't heard the door open or sensed she was there. He couldn't let anything distract him. Too much was at stake.

"Mama, you're up." Camy ran to her and threw her arms around Aubrey.

"Grandma is waiting for you both in the den."

As the two hurried through the kitchen into the hallway, Sean entered and closed the door then locked it. "Did you get some rest?"

"Yes, much better than at the hospital. The test will be tomorrow when I'm at the courthouse the whole day. I don't want any delays in this trial. Maybe when it's over, my life will get back to normal. Anything new at the burial ground?"

"No one else has been found since this morning. I hope Jack is the last body. Nine will keep the police busy."

"Over how many years?"

"So far, the ME estimates about two and a half years."

"Right before Samuel was murdered. Any tips on the guy from the hospital?"

"No, but this afternoon the police were offering a reward for a tip that leads to the man's arrest." Sean followed Aubrey from the kitchen to her office.

"If we're talking about the case, I'd rather do it in here. Not as easy for Sammy to overhear anything. Thanks for saying something to him earlier, by the way. He can be quite competitive. Camy is my shy one, as I'm sure you've figured out. She doesn't try too many new things, whereas Sammy will try anything. He was most likely competing in the womb for the last three months, so he could be first out. There were nights I got little sleep because of the activity." She took a seat on the couch and smiled. "I hadn't thought about that in years."

"I have a couple of nephews and one niece from my older sister," Sean said. "Both of my sisters live in Amarillo. I go back home a couple times a year."

"So you aren't a novice with kids?"

"No." He sat across from her.

"I'm an only child. My dad left when I was six, and Mama went back to work as a nurse. I stayed with the next-door neighbor in Galveston when she was working. My best friend lived there." She looked at her folded hands in her lap. "I didn't bring you in here to talk about our childhoods, though. I've been thinking about what you said about notes or something like that concerning the couple of days my husband worked on your brother's disappearance. Samuel wrote down everything in a notepad. He went through one a month. I turned over what I found to you, but maybe the most recent one wasn't in that batch. What date did they end?"

"On the case before Jack. He still had some blank pages, so I thought he hadn't gotten anything to put in his notes."

"I'm assuming you read through them to see what's been going on here. How would you describe the notes?"

"Detailed."

"You got everything from in here. Mama dealt with the bedroom. A lot of it went into the attic. When the kids get older, they might be interested in Samuel's items. It's time I go through them. Mama didn't throw anything away, so there are things in there that won't be of interest to Sammy and Camy. I need to weed them out anyway. It gets hot in the attic, so if you can bring the boxes down, I'll go through them in here. I don't want my children to see them until I look through his belongings. What do you think about doing that in the evenings after they go to bed? We'll access the attic through the garage."

"Sounds good. How many containers are we talking about?"

She remembered taking them up to the attic—a two-week-long project with two toddlers underfoot who wanted her attention. "I estimate there are about sixty or seventy boxes filled with his things from the whole house. I kept some of his clothes, but the majority was given to a homeless shelter. Similar to his notes, he liked to keep everything just in case he might need it later. I'm the opposite. I don't like clutter, but with children you often end up with some."

"I don't see that many boxes being stacked in this room. I'll start with ten, look through them then put the cartons back in the attic, so if your twins somehow discover them in here, it won't seem that unusual. What do you think?"

"That makes sense, because Sammy has snuck in here before. If he found out it was his dad's stuff, he'd want to go through every box."

"That's what I figured. Very inquisitive. Good skills for a law enforcement officer."

She frowned. "I have many years to sway him toward an appropriate job."

"I thought he wanted to be a Texas Ranger like his dad."

"He does. But I lost my husband to the job. I don't want to lose Sammy to it, too."

"We can't control death. Life is full of risks, some unexpected. When it's my time, then so be it. When I started as a law enforcement officer, I made a pact with myself. I wouldn't worry about death. That didn't mean I would do reckless things to tempt it. Instead I turned it over to the Lord. He's in control. Once I accepted that, it gave me a calm, free feeling. Think what would happen if we didn't have laws and the police to enforce them. Complete chaos. I refuse to live like that."

"I believe in the law, too. I'm a judge. And what you said is true. I just don't want to have my child follow in his father's footsteps. There are other things he could do that will help people but be safer. Look at the rising deaths of law enforcement officers."

He wanted to argue more, convince her that being a police officer didn't mean getting killed. "That's why I turned it over to the Lord. Each time I go out on a call, if I think about being killed, I wouldn't be able to do my job. I need to remain focused, not be distracted. That's when things can go wrong."

"I wish I could. But it's not that easy." Aubrey rose and stretched. "I'm going to check on my children."

He hung back. He couldn't blame her for what she felt. She'd lost her husband. Remembering back to his childhood, he knew what a husband's death could do to a family. It had left his mother struggling to make ends meet and to do the job of raising her children by herself. Had he kept part of himself back from the women he'd dated because he was in a job that could be dangerous?

What had made her say those words about Sammy not being a law enforcement officer when he grew up? She had a feeling when her son made a decision about doing a certain job, she wasn't going to be able to change his mind. He was as stubborn as she was. Her mother had tried to get Aubrey to become a nurse, but she wouldn't have anything to do with being one. The scent of blood made her nauseated, so how could she have a job in the medical field? She and her mama had had a few arguments over that, but in the end her mother couldn't change her mind.

When Aubrey entered the den, she immediately went over to where her children and Mama sat on the floor playing a game of War. She homeschooled her twins, and this game helped them to understand the value of different numbers. "Who's winning?"

Camy smiled. "I am."

Aubrey sat between her daughter and son, glancing at the entrance several times before Sean came into the den and took a place across from her.

"Who will play a game of War with me?" Sean glanced at each person in the circle, ending on Aubrey. One corner of his mouth tilted up, and he winked at her.

She chuckled. "Let's use two decks of cards and we can all play. *Abuela* will be the referee."

Camy's forehead crinkled. "What's that, Mama?"

"A referee makes sure everything is done right."

Aubrey's mother shuffled two decks of cards together then dealt them out. "Remember the rules for our version of War. Aces are number one, therefore the lowest number. The highest number wins. There are no jacks, queens and kings, and if there's a tie, you battle for all the cards. And last but not least, I'm setting the timer for fifteen minutes. Whoever has the most cards at the end of that time wins. There can be more than one winner."

Sean rubbed his hands together. "I'm ready to win."

Sammy followed suit. "No, I am!"

"Y'all are wrong. It will be me," Aubrey said with a laugh.

At the end of the game, Camy, the quiet one, jumped to her feet, clapping. "I won!"

Sean stood and carried Camy around the den on his shoulders. "The War champion."

Aubrey started clapping, then her mother and Sammy.

Camy smiled from ear to ear. This set the mood for the evening, from the children helping Sean and Aubrey with dinner and cleanup, to story time, with Sean acting out a story that Aubrey read to her twins. It ended with Sean carrying Camy upstairs to her room, asleep. While Aubrey removed her daughter's shoes and tucked her into bed, Sean went back downstairs to bring Sammy up.

After Aubrey kissed Camy good-night, she left and crossed the hallway to Sammy's room. She stood in the doorway. Sean had already gotten her son ready for bed. Sean kissed his forehead and straightened. When he turned, their gazes met.

Aubrey's heart swelled at the thought of how much fun the evening had been. She hadn't thought of the trial and situation she was in for the last couple of hours. It felt wonderful, but then she caught sight of the Texas Ranger star on his shirt and reality quickly returned full force. She tore her attention from Sean and closed the distance to her son. She bent over and kissed Sammy.

She left her son's room after Sean and pulled the door nearly closed, leaving a gap of two inches. She moved down the hallway with him, a thoughtful expression clouding his eyes.

"Is something wrong?" She touched his arm.

He stopped and twisted toward her. "I was just thinking about how much I miss seeing my niece and nephews. Tonight reminded me of the fun we used to have. I didn't realize I miss having children around."

"Sometimes you don't realize what's important until you lose it. Until now, I've taken for granted my freedom to move around as I want without having others with me to protect me or going places without having to assess what dangers lie ahead."

"You have more than yourself to consider."

"Being suspicious and cautious are a good part of your life, aren't they?"

"In some cases more than others."

"How do you live always assessing your surroundings, looking for something wrong?"

"It comes automatically after a while." He clasped her hands. "Right now, I'm aware of the stairs to the left of us, a window at each end of the hall, the bathroom wide-open, the kids' doors ajar and two bedrooms to my right, with one door closed and the other open. Since we brought Sammy and Camy upstairs, Camilla must have gone to her room."

"Because her door is shut?"

"Yes, and she dimmed the entry hall lights. She does that every night before going to bed."

"I never thought about that."

"You probably will from now on." His eyes lit up as he took in her face.

She inched closer and was comforted when he did, too.

"I've seen you in your courtroom at a trial. You're aware of everything going on. You're constantly scanning the room." He released one hand and slid his arm around her waist while dipping his head toward hers.

"I never thought about that, but I do. It's a habit."

"Right, a habit," he murmured close to her mouth. "It's not a bad one to have. Being vigilant can help save your life." His breath whispered across her lips, parting them slightly.

Every sense became aware of Sean.

*Kiss me.*

# SEVEN

*What am I doing?* Sean pulled back. He shouldn't kiss her, no matter how much he wanted to.

Aubrey curled her arm around the back of his neck and tugged him closer.

All common sense flew from his mind. Cupping her face, he kissed her. And for a few seconds, he forgot his surroundings.

A faint sound penetrated his mind. A door opening.

His training kicked in, and he quickly stepped back, looking right and left. Camilla went into the bathroom. He dropped his hands to his sides, heat flushing his cheeks.

When he looked at Aubrey, a blush tinted her face. "I need to go downstairs and make sure the house is locked up tight. See you in the morning." He turned to leave.

"Wait!"

He slanted a glance over his shoulder.

"I wanted you to kiss me."

"And I wanted to kiss you, but it's not the right time or place. Good night, Aubrey."

As he descended the stairs, he felt her gaze on him.

There was a part of him that wanted to go back up the steps and really kiss her.

He didn't, but the thought stayed with him as he went through the house making sure every door and window were locked. He'd never worked a case where he'd wanted to, as the saying went, throw caution to the wind. Aubrey's life as well as her children's and her mother's were at stake. But her own words earlier concerning the dangerous nature of his job told him it would never work out between them.

He switched off the alarm and opened the front door. Every night he touched base with the officer on duty outside on the porch, then went out back to check on the one now assigned to the backyard. After they'd talked at the burial ground today, the police chief decided an extra guard at night at Aubrey's home would be a good precaution. Sean had agreed readily when he left and turned back to look at the burial ground from a distance. The sight indicated that the cartel wanted to control and quiet people.

Now Officer Cal Adams was on the porch and Officer Johnston, new to the guard duty, was on the patio.

"I'm going to bed. I'll let you know each night. The judge has an alarm system that's on all the time. It's connected to the doors and windows. Did Chief Perez give you my cell phone number?"

The young man nodded.

"Good. Thank you."

Sean went back into the house, feeling better that there were two officers on duty.

As he lay on the couch, he couldn't shake his thoughts of staring down at his brother's grave this morning. He still needed to call his two sisters, now that the identification was confirmed by the X-ray of Jack's arm.

The buried pain rose into Sean's throat, jamming it. He rolled over onto his side and pounded his pillow as if that would release his frustration and anger. *Lord, I don't think I can forgive the guy who murdered my brother. I'm determined to find him and make him pay for what he did.*

On Wednesday night, Aubrey sat on the floor in her office with a carton of Samuel's items in front of her.

Sean entered the room, carrying a couple of boxes. "I thought we could go through two more before calling it a day."

She almost moaned but managed to keep it inside.

Sean touched her arm. "After these we only have thirty to go through. We're moving fast. I think we can do the rest tomorrow night. You need to call it a night. I'll finish these. It won't take me long."

"No, I should have done this two years ago. As I'm going through his stuff, I'm reliving good and bad memories. A few have made me realize I'm still holding on to anger at my husband for putting his life in danger. The couple of months before his death, he did things he didn't normally do. The last few days were even worse. He wasn't getting any sleep. He got angry at everything. The morning of the day he died, he yelled at the kids for making a mess eating at the kitchen table. That wasn't like him."

"Do you think it was because of the case he was working on?"

She thought back to the last days with Samuel. Even for him, he'd been unusually silent—even troubled more than usual. Why? Would looking back finally give her answers to her questions?

"Possibly, especially if it had to do with the Coastal Cartel."

"There are some things that are hard to talk about. Recently Texas Ranger Dallas Sanders discovered a baby-kidnapping ring near San Antonio. His nephew was one of the babies stolen."

"I know about the case. I'm so glad the people behind it were convicted of kidnapping and trafficking. Do you think something like that is going on here?"

"Sadly, it's always a possibility. But a lot of my cases involve drugs, both illegal and legal ones, being sold unlawfully."

Her muscles stiff from sitting in the same position for an hour, Aubrey pushed to her feet and stretched her arms above her head then bent from side to side. After walking around the office, she resumed her place in front of one of the bigger cartons. "Remind me tomorrow to get up and move around after every box."

"I'll let you take the boxes back to the attic if you want."

The impish grin on his face fixed her attention on him for a moment. "You have bigger muscles than I do. I'll let you keep doing that part."

He chuckled. "At least I'm not stiff."

As he continued going through the items, Aubrey again focused on what was before her. A lot of the box's contents were from Samuel's days at the University of Texas.

She picked up the *Cactus* yearbook from Samuel's senior year and flipped through the pages until she found where she'd written a note in it. They had met when he was a senior and she a freshman. She'd known at the beginning how special Samuel was, although they didn't marry until her senior year. Now she wished she had wed earlier. He'd wanted to, but she'd been cautious. How could she have fallen in love with him after only knowing him a short time? She'd seen so many marriages fall apart because the couple rushed like her parents had, and their union ended in a divorce when she was six. They had dated only four months before getting married.

"Aubrey, is something wrong?"

She blinked at the page she'd been staring at, closed the yearbook and put it to the side. "I'm fine."

Quickly she reached into the carton and grabbed the first thing she touched. She picked up Samuel's wallet. She remembered getting it back from the police—instead of looking at it, she'd tossed it into the nearest carton her mother was filling. It had been in Samuel's back pocket and water drenched. The police had gone through it. There might be something her children might want to keep. She pulled out his driver's license, Texas Ranger identification card, a credit card that she'd canceled immediately, medical insurance card and photos of the twins and her. The pictures were damaged by water—Samuel had been found submerged in a river—but the other items were plastic and in good condition.

She decided to empty the worn leather wallet and throw it away. As she did, she felt something behind a picture of her, under a flap. She tugged on the piece of leather until she revealed a thin key. It looked like their safety-deposit key, but when she saw the number etched into the metal, it was different from the one they had.

Aubrey held it up. "This is a safety-deposit box key, but not one I know about."

Sean looked up. Hope flared in his expression. "You didn't have a second one?"

She shook her head. "It could be one at our bank, but not the one I used. I'll go get the key I have, and we can compare." She stood and sat in her chair behind the desk, then pulled open the top drawer. After feeling around, she located the key taped to the wood and held it up. "Not the same. This one has one hole punched in it. The other has three."

The corners of Sean's mouth turned downward. "I was hoping it was the same. Finding the safety-deposit box will be harder, but not impossible. Tomorrow I'll start with the banks in this area and find out what their keys look like. Any that have the three holes, we'll investigate."

"I didn't sign anything for a second safety-deposit box, so possibly a court order might be involved. If that's the case, it shouldn't be a problem. I know several judges who would grant one under the circumstances. Going through the courts may take a while, though."

"Hopefully I can find the bank tomorrow and get things rolling."

"Should we go through the rest of the boxes?"

"Yes. I'll finish up in here. I can see the toll this is taking on you."

She brought the key to Sean. "It's not so much the contents of the cartons. It's only been four days since I was poisoned. After a full day in court, I'm more exhausted than usual."

"I'll do the bulk tomorrow night, and Friday morning if I have anything, I'll show you."

She hated not finishing the task. She had to admit going through Samuel's possessions helped her come to terms with his death better than anything she'd done in the past two years. And having Sean here made it even easier than she thought it would be. In a short time, she felt a bond with him.

"Thanks for finishing up in here tonight. Tomorrow will be a full day with the prosecution calling more people to testify. So far, their case is solid."

Sean rose.

"I can go upstairs by myself."

"I know. But I'm going to check all the doors and windows again, even the ones on the second floor."

"My alarm would have gone off if anyone tried to breach one."

"Humor me. In my years as a law enforcement officer, I've seen some things that people didn't think was possible."

"Where there's a will, there's a way."

He nodded. "To be truthful, I like walking you to your room. But this time, I'll stand by the staircase."

"Why? You can't check the windows and doors if you stay there."

His cheeks flushed. "I must remain professional. I don't want anything to stand in the way of that. I've seen personal feelings cause problems on a case."

"By you?"

He shook his head. "It could, though, with this one. Partially because of my brother, but—" his gaze snagged hers "—mostly because of you. I'll feel better making sure you're all right when you go to your room, then I'll recheck the kids' rooms."

She had to force herself not to smile at his plan. It

was important to him. The implication of his words and their brief kiss last night caused flutters in her stomach. As she left her office with Sean a few feet behind her, she couldn't contain the grin, but she kept him from seeing her reaction.

At the top of the staircase, she walked a few feet down the hall, stopped and turned. "I'm checking on Sammy and Camy before I go to bed, so you won't have to."

When she went into Camy's bedroom, lit by a dim night-light, she checked the window, glancing out and spotting the police officer on the patio. In less than a week, her life and her family's had been turned upside down.

After she came out of her son's room, she walked past Sean. "Good night."

He caught her hand and stopped her. "The trial won't last too much longer, then your life should return to normal. I think the cartel is trying to delay the trial until they can find the key witness being guarded by the US Marshals."

"I hope it's over when the trial is. That's why I came back for a full day today rather than half like my doctor advised."

His eyebrows rose. "Why didn't you tell me that?"

"Because you would try to persuade me to do what he said. I want this trial wrapped up by the end of next week."

"So do I. Then I can work totally on my brother's and your husband's murders. See you tomorrow morning."

When she entered her room and closed the door, the long day finally blanketed her in total exhaustion. Sitting on her bed, she checked the monitors of her children's rooms to make sure they were turned on and working. Then she lay back and stared at the dark ceiling.

As tired as she was, her mind continued to swirl with her walk down memory lane. So many items she'd gone through brought back memories—but the main one was how her husband had changed in the last months of his life. Why?

Dressed as a Texas Ranger on Thursday afternoon, Sean exited the third bank in the region with safety-deposit boxes with the type of key he had. He had one more bank left before he would have to broaden the search perimeter. Why did Samuel have a secret safety-deposit box? Was it involved with something he had been working on? Or items he'd wanted hidden from Aubrey?

Earlier he'd talked to her while she was eating lunch in her office. The defense attorney was trying to delay the trial as much as he could—asking the same question in different ways or objecting to every little thing.

Sean slipped into the driver's seat, switched on his engine and backed out of the parking space. He wanted to be at the courthouse in the next hour. Although they had the mysterious safety-deposit box key, there could be something else in the remaining cartons that could help him figure out what was going on with the attacks against Aubrey.

Sean pulled into a place right in front of the Port Bliss Bank and climbed from his SUV. He asked an employee to let him into his safety-deposit box, number 833.

While the young woman withdrew the card for that box and wrote down the time, Sean glanced at the name of the account holder—Bryan Madison. This could be the one. She handed him a pen and slid the signature card in his direction.

She suddenly stopped. "Oh, I forgot. I need to see your driver's license."

Although he'd already seen the name of the box holder, he acted like he'd seen Bryan Madison on the card for the first time. "That's not my account. I'm Sean McNair. I must have the wrong branch. It's been a couple of years, and I just forgot which one. Sorry, ma'am. I need to go to the one on Houston Street."

He backed away a few feet then pivoted and marched to the exit. He'd already gone through the same routine at the branch on the highway into town. He wondered if Samuel's middle name was Bryan. That explained why the account hadn't been sealed by the bank when Samuel Madison died. If he was right about this being the safety-deposit box, at least now he wouldn't have to search more banks, and as soon as Aubrey could get a court order to open the box, they might have evidence to help her get answers concerning Samuel's death.

Aubrey should be ready to leave the courthouse soon. After he drove into the rear parking lot, he walked toward the back entrance into the building, noting the deputy sheriff on duty outside in the lot. Halfway to the building, the door flung open and people began hurrying out of the courthouse.

Something was wrong. It had to be connected to Villa's trial. The word *bomb* flitted through his mind as he raced toward the building. The door was a bottleneck, making it hard for him to get inside. Even outside, he heard a voice over the loudspeaker telling everyone to move calmly to the exits.

Finally in the hallway, Sean spied Deputy Lockhart nearby. He pushed against the tide of the crowd and reached the older man. "What's going on?"

"Someone called to say there was a bomb in the courthouse."

"Have you seen Judge Madison?"

"Not yet."

He continued weaving his way through the crowd. The front exit was the nearest one for Aubrey's courtroom. When the crush of people surrounding him lessened, he pulled out his phone and called Aubrey.

It rang until it went to voice mail. "Call me. I'm on the first floor of the courthouse. Where are you?"

Not three seconds after he disconnected, his phone rang, and he quickly answered it, relieved it was Aubrey.

"I'm out front under the big oak tree. I have three deputy sheriffs surrounding me. When it happened, I dismissed the trial for the day."

"Do the deputies know what's going on?"

"One's on the phone with the sheriff."

"I'll be there shortly."

As the throng leaving the building thinned out, Sean increased his pace. On the front steps outside, he paused and assessed the area. Police officers were arriving, joining the ones already at the scene. This could be an attempt against Aubrey, but more likely it had to do with Villa. Or it was a prank.

Spying Aubrey against the trunk of a big tree near the street, with the deputies standing in front of her, he hurried in her direction. He couldn't remember a previous bomb scare at the courthouse. As he approached, he caught sight of Aubrey's face when she moved slightly to the right. She saw him and smiled. Then one of the guards moved and blocked his view.

His heart racing, Sean stopped in front of the deputy sheriff in charge of Aubrey's detail. "What did Sheriff Bailey say?"

"He's on the way. Two bomb-detection dogs are coming soon to help the dog in the rear parking lot cover the building. Police Chief Perez just arrived and will be making an announcement soon."

Sean peered between two guards and spoke to Aubrey. "We're leaving. I'm going to get my SUV. Until I come back, stay here. I'll call to let you know where I am."

She nodded.

"We'll get her to your car. The east side would be the closest," the deputy sheriff said.

"If I don't think it's safe, I'll move to where it is and let you know." Sean threw Aubrey one last glance, then started toward the east side of the courthouse, keeping his eye on anything that might be suspicious.

In the background, the police chief came over a PA system and told the people to leave the courthouse grounds, which would be shut down for the rest of the day while it was being cleared. No unauthorized people would be allowed inside today. As the crowd continued to quickly disperse, Sean lost sight of Aubrey. He reconsidered his plan with the evacuation of everyone in the building causing a massive mob clogging the streets, which would further hamper him getting Aubrey to safety. It would be easy for a killer to mix with the throng and try to kill Aubrey—if that was his target. He wouldn't take that risk.

As he retraced his steps back to Aubrey, he rethought his plan. He'd feel better if Aubrey was under his protection in this situation. As a Texas Ranger, he owed Samuel that much.

When he reached the deputy sheriffs and Aubrey, Sean traded places with one of the deputies, putting himself in front of her. "I need you to get my SUV and bring it around to a safe spot, then let us know." He handed the man his keys, described his car and where it was parked. "I realize this will take longer because of all these people. I don't want Aubrey in the middle of the crowd."

The deputy sheriff quickly disappeared among the people leaving and those responding to the bomb threat.

Sean kept his attention on the crowd while saying, "Are you all right?"

"I'm okay. I just called Mama to let her know I was outside a good distance from the courthouse, and nothing has gone off so far. Officer Carter told her about the bomb threat. I'm glad I could reassure her I was fine. But I'll feel better when I get home."

As he scanned every site that might work for a sniper, he was conscious of Aubrey being right behind him, her body occasionally brushing against his back as she shifted her weight. "Take off your black robe and give it to me. When we start for my car, I don't want you wearing it. The robe could make you stand out."

She shrugged out of it. "What do you want me to do with it?"

"Leave it on the ground. I'll have Deputy Worth

come back for it." Sean looked at the law enforcement officer. "Is Villa safe?"

"Yes, he's back at the county jail instead of his cell at the courthouse."

"Good. I was afraid this could be an attempt to break him out." Or, if there was an internal war starting within the cartel, an attempt to kill Villa.

When the deputy sheriff in charge of the escort received a call from the one who'd gone to pick up Sean's car, Aubrey tensed. So close to her, Sean could feel it ripple down her body.

"Stay right by my side," he said, taking hold of her elbow.

On her left and slightly behind her, Deputy Worth fell into step with Aubrey. The deputy in charge led the way toward the west side of the courthouse. When his SUV came into sight, Sean increased the pace while keeping an eye on their surroundings. The crowd was starting to thin out, finally.

After they reached his vehicle and Aubrey settled into the front passenger seat, Sean hurried around to the driver's-side door and climbed into the car. "I'm taking a different route to your place."

"I never thought there were so many ways to drive to my home from the courthouse," Aubrey said with a forced laugh.

He glanced at her. "It's a talent I have." Then he pulled away from the curb and drove in the opposite direction of her house. He checked to make sure one of the deputy sheriffs was following them in an un-marked car. "I have good news. I think I found the safety-deposit box, and all we'll need is a court order."

"When I get home, I'll call Judge Rodriquez. What name is it under, and which bank?"

"Bryan Madison at the downtown Port Bliss Bank."

"That's got to be him. Bryan is Samuel's middle name. Maybe what's inside the box will help you with the investigation."

"How did Villa seem today when it was announced to evacuate the courthouse?"

"Arrogant. He quickly covered it, but I don't think he was behind the bomb threat. His brief glimpse of surprise wasn't fake."

Sean stopped at a four-way stop sign and slanted a look toward Aubrey. "That reinforces what my informant told me about a cleaner coming here to straighten everything out."

"Have you told the prosecutor about that?"

"Not yet. I wanted to corroborate the information as best I could first. But I will now when we get to your house. I know they've been pressing Villa on turning in members of the Coastal Cartel in the United States. So far he's refused to say anything." After Sean pulled into the driveway and parked his SUV inside the garage, he finally relaxed as the door came down.

Aubrey leaned back and closed her eyes, releasing a long breath. "It's good to be home."

"Before the bomb threat, how were things going in the trial?"

"Slow. As I've mentioned, the defense is stonewalling." She opened her eyes and sat up. "I wouldn't put it past the defense attorney to arrange for the bomb threat."

"It's possible, but I think the cartel is more likely. The sheriff will call me when they've okayed the court-

# "4 for 4" MINI-SURVEY

We are prepared to **REWARD** you with 4 FREE books and Free Gifts for completing our MINI SURVEY!

**Romance**

**Suspense**

You'll get up to...

**4 FREE BOOKS & FREE GIFTS**

*FREE* Value Over **$20!**

just for participating in our Mini Survey!

# Get Up To 4 Free Books!

Dear Reader,

**IT'S A FACT:** if you answer 4 quick questions, we'll send you 4 FREE REWARDS from each series you try!

Try **Love Inspired® Romance Larger-Print** books featuring Christian characters facing modern-day challenges.

Try **Love Inspired® Suspense Larger-Print** novels featuring Christian characters facing challenges to their faith... and lives

## Or **TRY BOTH!**

I'm not kidding you. As a leading publisher of women's fiction, we value your opinions... and your time. That's why we are prepared to reward you handsomely for completing our mini-survey. In fact, we have 4 Free Rewards for you, including 2 free books and 2 free gifts from each series you try!

Thank you for participating in our survey,

*Pam Powers*

www.ReaderService.com

# To get your 4 FREE REWARDS:
## Complete the survey below and return the insert today to receive up to 4 FREE BOOKS and FREE GIFTS guaranteed!

▼ DETACH AND MAIL CARD TODAY! ▼

## "4 for 4" MINI-SURVEY

**1** Is reading one of your favorite hobbies?
☐ YES  ☐ NO

**2** Do you prefer to read instead of watch TV?
☐ YES  ☐ NO

**3** Do you read newspapers and magazines?
☐ YES  ☐ NO

**4** Do you enjoy trying new book series with FREE BOOKS?
☐ YES  ☐ NO

Please send me my Free Rewards, consisting of **2 Free Books from each series I select** and **Free Mystery Gifts**. I understand that I am under no obligation to buy anything, as explained on the back of this card.

❏ **Love Inspired® Romance Larger-Print** (122/322 IDL GNPV)
❏ **Love Inspired® Suspense Larger-Print** (107/307 IDL GNPV)
❏ **Try Both** (122/322/107/307 IDL GNP7)

|  |  |
|---|---|
| FIRST NAME | LAST NAME |

ADDRESS

|  |  |
|---|---|
| APT.# | CITY |

|  |  |
|---|---|
| STATE/PROV. | ZIP/POSTAL CODE |

Offer limited to one per household and not applicable to series that subscriber is currently receiving. **Your Privacy**—The Reader Service is committed to protecting your privacy. Our Privacy Policy is available online at www.ReaderService.com or upon request from the Reader Service. We make a portion of our mailing list available to reputable third parties that offer products we believe may interest you. If you prefer that we not exchange your name with third parties, or if you wish to clarify or modify your communication preferences, please visit us at www.ReaderService.com/consumerschoice or write to us at Reader Service Preference Service, P.O. Box 9062, Buffalo, NY 14240-9062. Include your complete name and address. LI/SLI-219-MSPC18

© 2018 HARLEQUIN ENTERPRISES LIMITED
® and ™ are trademarks owned and used by the trademark owner and/or its licensee. Printed in the U.S.A.

## READER SERVICE—Here's how it works:

Accepting your 2 free books and 2 free gifts (gifts valued at approximately $10.00 retail) places you under no obligation to buy anything. You may keep the books and gifts and return the shipping statement marked "cancel." If you do not cancel, approximately one month later we'll send you 6 more books from each series you have chosen, and bill you at our low, subscribers-only discount price. Love Inspired® Romance Larger-Print books and Love Inspired® Suspense Larger-Print books consist of 6 books each month and cost just $5.74 each in the U.S. or $6.24 each in Canada. That is a savings of at least 18% off the cover price. It's quite a bargain! Shipping and handling is just 50¢ per book in the U.S. and 75¢ per book in Canada*. You may return any shipment at our expense and cancel at any time — or you may continue to receive monthly shipments at our low, subscribers-only discount price plus shipping and handling. *Terms and prices subject to change without notice. Prices do not include sales taxes which will be charged (if applicable) based on your state or country of residence. Canadian residents will be charged applicable taxes. Offer not valid in Quebec. Books received may not be as shown. All orders subject to approval. Credit or debit balances in a customer's account(s) may be offset by any other outstanding balance owed by or to the customer. Please allow 3 to 4 weeks for delivery. Offer available while quantities last.

▲ If offer card is missing write to: Reader Service, P.O. Box 1341, Buffalo, NY 14240-8531 or visit www.ReaderService.com ▲

**BUSINESS REPLY MAIL**
FIRST-CLASS MAIL     PERMIT NO. 717     BUFFALO, NY

POSTAGE WILL BE PAID BY ADDRESSEE

**READER SERVICE**
PO BOX 1341
BUFFALO NY 14240-8571

NO POSTAGE
NECESSARY
IF MAILED
IN THE
UNITED STATES

house. It can be a long process to clear a three-story building."

"I hope we can meet tomorrow. I don't want to take any time off. I want my life back."

"I'm with you on that. Ready to go inside?"

She nodded. "After I hug my children, I'll call Judge Rodriquez about signing a court order to open Bryan Madison's safety-deposit box."

Before he had a chance to open the door into the utility room, it burst wide-open. Sean jumped back as Sammy and Camy ran out of the house, throwing their arms around Aubrey.

"Mama, you're home." Camy looked up at her. "I missed ya."

She bent over and kissed Camy's forehead, then Sammy's.

"Can we go outside?" the little boy asked.

Camilla appeared in the entrance. "Sammy, Camy, give them a chance to come inside."

Aubrey moved toward the doorway with both of her children clinging to her.

Sean ruffled her son's hair. "Are you ready to practice kicking the soccer ball into the net?"

The boy stopped and twisted around to face Sean. "Yes!"

"Then let me change, and we will. Camy, do you want to do it, too?"

In the kitchen, Camy nodded with a big grin on her face.

Sean left the room, grabbed his duffel bag and changed into shorts and a T-shirt in the downstairs bathroom. He needed the exercise. After the bomb threat at the courthouse, he felt wound tight. While

Aubrey was in court tomorrow, he hoped to drive to Brownsville to track down another informant and see what information he could get from him. If he said the same as his other one in Port Bliss, then today was the opening move. He didn't like leaving town, even if it would only be for three or four hours, but this informant was a member of the cartel. Meeting him would be trickier.

When he returned to the kitchen, the twins were at the door waiting. Camilla was getting ingredients out of the refrigerator for dinner. "What are you fixing tonight?"

"I promised Camy we'd have macaroni and cheese. I make it from scratch."

"I don't think I've had that in years. Sounds great."

Camy clapped her hands. "Yay! It's my favorite."

"Let's work up an appetite." Sean opened the door, and Aubrey's two kids darted outside, racing for the soccer ball in the middle of the yard. Sean paused at the chair where the police officer sat. "Anything unusual today?"

"Other than the children knocking on that window—" he pointed his thumb at it "—it's been quiet. I heard about the bomb threat. I'm glad nothing happened."

"Me, too."

Sean jogged toward Sammy and Camy, who were playing tug-of-war with the ball.

"I got here first," Camy said.

"No, I did." Sammy yanked hard on the ball, but his sister held on.

Sean stepped closer and towered over the two children. They stopped and looked up at him. Wearing his stern face, Sean held out his hands, and they both gave him the soccer ball. "In soccer, unless you're the goalie, you don't touch the ball while playing on the field. We're going to put our hands behind our backs—" he demonstrated "—and pass the ball to each other. Like this." He showed them what to do.

Twenty minutes later, Camy and Sammy had managed to keep their hands behind their backs and kick the ball more than two feet.

Camy leaped up and down. "I did it!"

Shortly after that Sammy did, too. He high-fived Sean. Then Camy had to do it. Right after that, she hugged him. Her brother quickly joined her. A lump rose in his throat as he remembered wanting to be a father. His own had been supportive and caring, but Sean had let Jack down. He had to find out what happened to him. He owed Jack that much.

Aubrey sat up in her bed and glanced at the digital clock on her nightstand. Six in the morning. She was wide-awake an hour early. She lay back down, closed her eyes and tried to empty her mind. But all she could think about was yesterday and Sean. When he'd arrived under the large oak tree at the courthouse, she'd finally relaxed. She'd known she would be all right.

Then last night, she and Sean finally finished going through Samuel's belongings and found nothing else. After putting the boxes back up in the attic, they wrote a court order for opening the box at the bank. She talked with Judge Rodriquez, and she and Sean would meet him before Villa's trial tomorrow. What had Samuel put in the safety-deposit box?

The question wouldn't leave her mind. She sat up again and decided to get ready for work early. Late last night she'd heard from the sheriff that the courthouse was safe to return to. They found a bomb in a bag, and it was deactivated and removed. The sheriff was working on how it came in and who brought it into the building. In the meantime, he reassured her that security would be tightened even more.

She stood and stretched, then walked to the window to see what the weather looked like. When she opened the blinds, dawn streaked rich colors through the sky. She started to turn and go into the bathroom. But something out of the corner of her eye caught her attention in the dim light. She leaned her head against the glass pane, her fingernails digging into the window ledge.

*What is on the ground by the patio?*

# EIGHT

Aubrey raced from her bedroom to the living room, her heart beating so fast her breath came in short spurts. Before she reached Sean sleeping on the couch, he shot straight up.

His gaze immediately fixed on her. "What's wrong?"

"I'm not sure. I couldn't see much from my angle."

He stood, his brow furrowed. "See what? Where?"

Aubrey lifted her trembling hand and pointed toward the kitchen. "Patio. I think someone's down on the ground."

Sean grabbed his gun from under his pillow and rushed through the dining room into the kitchen. "Turn off the alarm."

Aubrey took care of the security system, then followed Sean. Had something happened to the police officer? When she entered the kitchen, Sean was halfway out the door. She hurried after him.

He stopped and turned toward her. "I don't want you out here. Let the officer on the porch know that Officer Adams is down and to call 911. But he needs to stay out front, and you need to stay inside."

Aubrey did as Sean said. Officer Watkins, who usually stood guard on the porch, called for assistance while she shut the front door and locked it. Then she returned to the kitchen and watched from the bay window.

Sean partially blocked the view of the police officer on the ground, but she noticed his leg move. *Cal has a chance. Thank You, Lord.*

As Sean moved slightly to the right, Aubrey finally saw where Cal had been shot. Sean held his T-shirt over the right side of the officer's upper torso, trying to stem the flow of blood from the wound. Aubrey wanted to go outside and help, but she was the reason Cal was down. She didn't want anyone else hurt because somebody was after her. How did it happen? Why didn't she hear it? Her bedroom window had a view of the backyard, although part of the patio was out of sight from her room.

When the paramedics arrived, Sean stepped away so they could attend to Cal. Shortly after they came, two uniform police officers walked around the side of the house and headed for Sean while the EMTs transferred Cal to a gurney and wheeled him away. She had to do something to keep herself busy until Sean returned with news. She made a pot of coffee, then began pacing from one end of the kitchen to the other.

Her children had played outside in the backyard yesterday evening with Sean. They could have been shot. She had to do something more to protect her twins. Their home wasn't safe anymore, even with three law enforcement officers guarding them.

Finally, Sean entered the kitchen and locked the door, a grim expression on his face. "Adams is being transported to the hospital. I think he'll be all right."

She halted and turned toward him. "Where are the other two officers?"

"Inspecting the yard. I need to go out there and help, but I wanted to make sure you're okay."

"No, I'm not." Her hands shook so much she clasped them together in front of her. "My kids and mother aren't safe here at all. Someone shot one of the guards. What's going to stop them from storming the house? Everyone I love is in here." Tears blurred her vision and rolled down her cheeks.

He covered the distance between them and wrapped his arms around her. "I won't let that happen."

"You didn't hear the shot. I didn't. Was it a gun with a silencer?"

"Yes." He leaned back and looked into her eyes. "He should make it."

"When did this happen?"

"Probably about thirty minutes ago, right before dawn. He hit his head and blacked out. When I went out there, he was regaining consciousness but still groggy. He was taking his walk around the yard when it happened. A squirrel scampered across the grass, and he turned toward it. That's what saved him from being hit in the heart."

She closed her eyes, trying to stem the flow of her tears. Cal could have died—protecting her.

"Chief Perez is on his way. The backyard will be scoured for any evidence. They'll figure out where the shot came from. I called for another Texas Ranger to come help."

"My children and mother aren't safe even here." She stepped back, shaking her head. "We've got to do something else."

"Even though Officer Adams was shot, whoever shot him didn't get into the house. Although we didn't hear the shot, we would have heard the alarm go off if the shooter had tried to get inside. If the shooter's objective was to get into your home, he would have done it earlier, before the sun started coming up. No, there might be another reason for what happened."

"Still, I don't want my children exposed to even the chance of being hurt. Maybe Mama can take them somewhere far away from here." Chewing on her thumbnail, Aubrey started pacing again, trying to come up with a place that would be safe for her family. At the moment her mind was blank, which sent her frustration level skyrocketing. She loved being a judge, but not at the risk of her family.

Sean moved into her path, stopping her. "I have an idea of where your children and mother can go."

"Where?"

"To Amarillo. My sister and her husband are police officers there, and they can protect them, with the support of the Texas Ranger in the area. The distance from here will help. I'll put in a request for a charter plane to take them there. If that isn't possible, then we can drive the thirteen hours to Amarillo. It will take me some time to set it up, but we should be able to leave either later today or tomorrow."

"I'm going with them. It'll be the weekend soon. I need to see them settled in a safe place."

"I figured you would say that. After I take you to the courthouse and go by the bank to pick up the items in the safety-deposit box, I'll come back here to work out the details of the trip and look over what was in Samuel's box. I'll be at your house most of the day. Call me at lunch, and I'll let you know what I've worked out."

"Let me know how Cal is." Aubrey tried to relax. Her children and mother would be up soon, and she didn't want them to know what was going on. But she couldn't ease the tension.

"I will. Don't let anyone know our plans. This will be between us and my major. The fewer people who know our plans, the better."

The sound of footsteps coming down the stairs drifted to her. "My children are up. Try to keep what happened from them. With you here most of the day, they'll want to go outside to play. They can't."

"I agree. I'll think of something to keep them entertained."

Sammy burst into the kitchen with Camy not far behind him. "Mama, more police out front. Can I go see if they'll let me turn on their siren?"

"No. Some people are sleeping still, and we don't need to wake up our neighbors."

"But—"

Aubrey quickly cut him off. "I need to get ready for work. Don't pester Sean about it." She hurried from the room before her son could say something else. Besides, she needed to get upstairs and explain what had happened in the backyard to her mama.

As she approached her mother's bedroom, she tried to come up with a way to tell her about Cal being shot and the need to leave here. It wouldn't be easy, especially because she didn't know why a shooter had tried to kill Cal. Sean was right. The alarm going off would have stopped the man from getting far into her house. How was Cal being shot going to stop Villa's trial?

* * *

A short time later, Sean and Aubrey left Judge Ro-driquez's chambers with the court order to open the safety-deposit box. "I'm going to the bank right after I leave the courthouse. I'm going to talk to the security office to get details about the bomb threat yesterday. I noticed the security at the entrances is much tighter."

"I'm having everyone who comes into my court be checked again. I'm not taking a chance, even though they'll be searched at the main doors, too. The other trials going on aren't high-profile like Villa's."

When they reached her office, two deputy sheriffs stood guard outside. Even with them in place, Sean went inside first and searched the whole chamber, then tested the door that led to the courtroom. It was locked. He opened it and looked into the short hallway. Empty. Once he felt there were no surprises for Aubrey, he escorted her inside and stayed while she readied her-self for the Villa trial, then he walked with her to the courtroom. The urge to hold her close to him and not let her go was strong.

He had to remind himself he was on duty and he'd done everything he could to keep her safe. As he left her chambers, a police officer and a dog came out of the room after checking where the trial was going to take place. The rest he had to put in God's hands.

Sean walked down the stairs to the first floor and crossed the lobby to the security office. When he en-tered, Sheriff Bailey was talking to the deputy sitting in front of a bank of screens showing different areas of the courthouse.

The sheriff glanced at Sean then tapped three of the screens. "Make sure you pay attention to the three entrances into the building. Until the Villa trial is completed, we've locked all doors in and out of here except these three—front, rear by the employee parking lot and the one on the west side where prisoners come into the courthouse near the holding cells. We have guards at all of them. We now have screening at the back and west doors like the front."

"Did you figure out which entrance the person who brought the bomb into the courthouse used?" Sean asked as another deputy entered the room and sat at the second chair in front of the security screens.

Sheriff Bailey shook his head. "The bag with the bomb was placed out of camera view. So far we haven't figured out how it was brought into the building."

"You think someone who works here is helping?"

"It's a definite possibility. We've added two bomb-detection dogs on the first floor continually making the rounds, as well as one dog on the second and another on the third floor. That's in addition to the one in the parking lot. I've had to call in a few favors for extra assistance."

"I noticed you have a couple deputies outside in the rear parking lot."

"I've been thinking about possible ways of getting a bomb in here unnoticed. The windows on the first floor open. Someone could have handed the bomb through one of them to an accomplice."

Sean nodded. "Good. We're dealing with the cartel, who have deep pockets. I'll be back later to pick up Judge Madison. If there's a problem, notify me right away."

When Sean drove out of the rear parking lot, he noted the guards on duty at its entrance and in the middle, as well as Deputy Lockhart and another he was familiar with at the back door. Sean headed for the Port Bliss Bank. He hoped there were answers inside the box, because he was beginning to wonder if all the incidents had to do with Villa's trial. He couldn't shake the feeling something wasn't right.

When he pulled into a parking space in front of the bank, he climbed from his vehicle and made his way inside. "I need to see the manager," he told the teller.

Her eyes grew round for a few seconds. She was the same one he'd talked to yesterday about the safety-deposit box. She gestured toward a short hallway. "Mr. Denton's office is there."

"Thank you, ma'am." He tapped the brim of his cowboy hat, then walked to the entrance she indicated and knocked on the door frame.

A short balding man glanced up from his computer. "May I be of help?"

Sean entered and closed the door, then crossed to the chair in front of the manager's desk. He gave the court order to the man. "I need to get into a safety-deposit box that's tied up in a case I'm working."

His forehead wrinkled, the bank manager read the court order, then pulled out his top drawer and withdrew a set of keys. "Come this way." He exited his office and glanced back at Sean a couple times as he went to the vault that held the boxes.

Mr. Denton put in both keys and turned them. He pulled out the safety-deposit box and put it on a viewing table, then he retreated out of the vault. Sean lifted the box's lid and peered inside. Only a black pad, like ones he used, lay on the bottom. He opened it and stared at the nonsense on the pages as he flipped through it. Was it written in a code?

He pocketed the notebook, closed the lid and went to find the manager. "This safety-deposit box needs to be sealed. Its owner is dead. I'll send you a death certificate."

"I'll take care of it."

Sean shook the manager's hand, then left the bank. He headed back to Aubrey's house to guard her family while he arranged for a plane to take them to Amarillo tonight or tomorrow. He hoped he could figure out what was in the notebook besides gibberish. Samuel wouldn't have gone to such lengths to hide it and keep it safe unless it was important. He hoped Aubrey could help. Could they crack the code before someone else was hurt?

Aubrey entered her chambers after a long day, even though she'd dismissed the court an hour earlier. Sean sat on her couch waiting for her. He greeted her with a smile and stood. The sight of him gave her a sense of peace in this trauma.

He had a plane arriving at the Galveston airport later tonight to take them to Amarillo. They would stay until Sunday morning to help her children adjust to the change, then the plane would return and take her and Sean back to Galveston. She hated being parted from Sammy and Camy, but at least her mother would be with them and they would be hundreds of miles away from Port Bliss and the danger here.

Sean walked toward her. "How did it go today?"

"Okay. I noticed today Villa wasn't himself. Usually he's confident and almost cocky. But not today. I understand the prosecution offered him another deal yesterday. Do you think the bomb threat had anything to do with this plea deal?"

"Like a clear message from Sanchez and the Coastal Cartel? Maybe. I haven't been able to contact my other informant to verify the appearance of a cleaner."

"Where's the notebook?"

He stuck his hand into his pocket, withdrew the pad and gave it to her. "I hope you understand what's written here."

She flipped through the pages. "I might be able to help. Samuel was fascinated with codes. I still have a couple of his books on different ones. We used to write messages in code to each other when we were dating."

Sean smiled. "Great. We'll take them with us and work on the notebook when we have time this weekend. We won't stay long at your house before leaving for Galveston."

"What if someone's watching my place? What if they follow us as we leave Port Bliss?"

"I have a plan. A couple of Texas Rangers along the route will check for anyone following us. The plane's destination will remain a secret. Your children and mother will be protected at a safe house in Amarillo. My sister and her husband will be there, as well as a Texas Ranger."

"Mama is making it sound like an adventure to the twins. It's what's best for them, but I'm going to miss them. We've never been apart since they were born, except when I was in the hospital last weekend."

"Let's go."

"Sheriff Bailey has really beefed up security at the courthouse. We had a bomb-detection dog go through my courtroom before everyone went in, then again after the lunch break. We can't let people intimidate us, but I won't lie and say I was perfectly fine, sitting in my chair pretending I was calm."

Sean put his hand at the small of her back and covered the distance to the door. "It's been a week. Hopefully the trial will be over by next Friday."

Out in the hall, one of the deputies followed them down the stairs to the first floor. At the rear door, the same two guards were posted as in the morning. She knew Bill, but the other was a new deputy to the courthouse. She could imagine the sheriff's resources were stretched, especially after the bomb threat yesterday.

"Have a good weekend, Judge Madison." Deputy Lockhart held the door open to her.

"Thanks, Bill. I hope you do, too."

"The trial will be over soon, and everything will get back to normal."

She smiled. "I've forgotten what normal means. See you Monday."

When she climbed into Sean's SUV, Aubrey collapsed back against the seat and closed her eyes, exhausted from intently watching over her courtroom and following the trial as it unfolded. And they still had to drive to Galveston and fly to Amarillo. At least her kids were excited because they got to fly on an airplane for the first time. She exhaled a long breath.

"Once the trial is over, Sammy and Camy will come back home." Sean sent her a grin as he pulled out of the parking lot into traffic.

Aubrey thought back to everything that had happened the past week. There were so many questions she couldn't answer. "Have you considered this might not have anything to do with the trial? Yes, the tactics so far have delayed the trial some, but more and more I think something else is going on."

"Yes, I have, but the bomb threat had to have been the cartel and something to do with Villa. I'm just not sure exactly why yet. If someone was just coming after you, why would he plant a bomb, and not even near your courtroom? It was left at the other end of the courthouse. The amount of explosives wouldn't have taken down the whole building. It would have mostly damaged a third of the first floor and possibly a small part of the second floor." He drove into her garage.

The sound of the garage door coming down used to make her feel safe, but with the shooting this morning, she realized this wasn't a safe haven anymore. "How is Cal?"

"He'll recover. His gunshot wound was a through and through. It didn't damage any vital organs."

"Good. I've been praying for him all day. Did the police figure out where the shot came from?"

"The trajectory is from a tree in the backyard of your neighbor behind you."

"The Richardsons' place?"

Sean nodded. "They're on a cruise out of Galveston and have been gone all week. From their next-door neighbor, the police discovered they won a trip recently."

"So this had been planned?"

"Maybe."

"Someone used their place to surveil my home?"

"The neighbor had a key to their house. Sergeant Daniels got permission from the owners to go in and look around an hour ago. He called to let me know that there's evidence someone had been in there."

Aubrey shivered and hugged her arms across her chest. "And we—*my kids*—went out in the backyard. If we hadn't already arranged to take them away, I would have now." She opened the passenger door. "Let's get the kids and Mama and get them to a safer place."

As she started to leave, Sean clasped her hand. "You'll be at a safe house, too. Only myself and a couple of Texas Rangers will know its location. No one else. You'll need to pack as though you're staying in Amarillo. And bring those code books for us to use."

His touch reminded her she wasn't alone in trying to figure out what was going on. When he slipped his hand away, she missed the connection. She exited the SUV, shaking her head slightly. Not too long ago her life had been so different. Now she was fighting to keep her family safe, do her duty as a judge and stay alive, all while attracted to a man who had the same job that had led to her husband's murder. Maybe with Camy, Sammy and Mama protected, Aubrey could sort through all the feelings emerging after mourning Samuel's death.

When she entered the house, the kitchen was empty. She'd expected her kids to be there the second they heard the garage door go up. They usually were. She glanced at Sean.

As though he could read her thoughts, Sean said, "They're probably excited and trying to help with the packing. I'd better help them. I'm already packed."

Aubrey and Sean mounted the stairs then strolled toward the children's bedrooms. When she peeked into Camy's room, she saw her daughter on the floor, trying to decide which toys to take with her. Aubrey crossed to Sammy's and chuckled at the sight of her son sitting on a suitcase, trying to zip the overstuffed bag.

Sammy looked up, his forehead crinkled. "The ball doesn't fit."

Behind her, Sean chuckled. "I've got an idea." He moved past Aubrey and approached her son. "You can carry the soccer ball."

Sammy peered up, his lower lip stuck out. "*Abuela* said I could only bring what fit in here. I *need* to practice."

Sean glanced back at her. "Go pack. I'll take care of this."

Aubrey hurried to her bedroom. Her mother already had a piece of large luggage on her bed, open and ready for her to fill.

For fifteen minutes she rushed from the closet to the dresser to the suitcase. When she finished packing, she heaved the bag off the bed and rolled it into the corridor. Before she forgot, she needed to get those books on code writing. Something important had to be in the notebook if Samuel had gone to all the trouble to protect it. She wished he had shared with her more about what was happening. But in the months leading up to his death, her husband had shut himself off from her.

She picked up her suitcase and carried it to her office. After choosing two books on the subject of codes, she took her luggage to the kitchen then started for the staircase to help her children. Her mother stood at the top with Camy next to her. Aubrey hurried up the steps to assist them.

Twenty minutes later, everyone was seated in the SUV with the bags in the back. Sean turned around to face the back seat. "Now let's go over this one more time. Camy and Sammy, sit on the floor and stay there until I say you can get up. Your mama is doing the same up in front. Your grandma will lie on the back seat. As soon as we're out of town, you'll be able to sit on the seat. Remember, only when I tell you. We're on a secret mission, and I don't want anyone to know we're leaving. Okay?"

Everyone said yes. Sammy was the only one grinning.

Sean faced forward while Aubrey squeezed herself between the dashboard and the seat. The garage door rose, and he backed out.

Aubrey prayed this worked. The police officers would guard an empty house until her family was at the safe place in Amarillo. Only a few law enforcement officers knew the whole plan. A couple of Texas Rangers were watching for any car following Sean's and relaying the information to him.

*Lord, we need Your protection. Please keep my family safe.*

Sean exited the plane in Amarillo and assessed his surroundings as he moved toward two SUVs. His sister and her husband climbed out of the lead vehicle.

He hurried his pace. "Claire, Thomas, it's so good to see y'all." He hugged his sister then shook hands with his brother-in-law.

Claire looked at the plane. "Where are the judge and her family?"

"I wanted to check that everything was safe before they got off." Sean turned his attention to the second

SUV. Two Texas Rangers left their vehicle. He knew both of them. "I'll go back and bring them here."

When he returned to the plane, their luggage was being removed from the back. He paused in the entrance and took another survey of the area. There was little activity at the airport in the middle of the night. He hoped it stayed that way. He wanted to slip into Amarillo unnoticed by anyone except his sister, her husband and the Texas Rangers. The fewer people who knew their whereabouts, the safer they would be.

"Are y'all ready to leave?" Sean stood at the front.

Camy, who had fallen asleep on the ride, yawned and stretched. Sammy hopped out of his chair and rushed toward Sean. To the four-year-old boy, this was a big adventure. On the plane, he'd stared out the window even though it was dark.

Sean stopped the boy by putting a hand on his shoulder before he flew by Sean and left the plane. "Whoa. We're all going to leave together. Stay right there."

Sammy tried to do what Sean said. The boy's feet stayed in place, but he leaned to the left and tried to peek out of the opening. When everyone was ready to go, Sean took Sammy's hand and escorted him off the airplane.

Sean introduced everyone to each other. Camy hid behind Aubrey, while Sammy stood right in front of Sean. He was glad he and Aubrey would be staying a day to help the kids feel comfortable.

After the luggage was loaded in the back of the second SUV, Thomas drove away from the airport with the two Texas Rangers following. "I think y'all will love the place where you're staying. It has an indoor pool."

Sammy clapped. "I love to swim."

"You won't go into the water without a life jacket on. You still have a lot to learn about swimming," Aubrey immediately said.

"How about you, Camy? Do you like swimming?" Sean asked, glad that they would be able to swim, which hopefully would keep the children from getting too antsy having to stay indoors the whole time.

The little girl nodded.

Half an hour later, they were settled into a large house. Sean wondered who owned the place, which sat on several acres outside Amarillo.

Texas Ranger Pierce Claiborne came up behind him as Sean looked around. "The government seized this house about eight months ago from a human-trafficking group that was caught. The members are now in prison. For the time being, it's being used as a safe house. The land around it is flat, so it's easy to see if anyone is approaching. The security system is excellent. Frank and I will be watching over them. Between your sister and brother-in-law and us, we won't let anything happen to them."

"Camy is shy, and Sammy is full of energy. He brought his soccer ball. He'll want to practice."

Pierce laughed. "I can handle him. Remember, I have a six-year-old son."

"I've done my duty. I've warned you."

Pierce clapped Sean on the back. "My friend, I think you really care about these kids."

"Yes. They're Samuel Madison's kids. I remember going to a seminar, and he was there not long after the twins were born. I saw probably a hundred photos of them that weekend." That was the first time he'd seen a picture of Aubrey. She was in a number of the photos.

After running through the house, the children helped take their suitcases to the large bedroom they were sharing with twin beds. Camilla would be staying in the room next to theirs while his sister and her husband were across the hall. Pierce would stay at the house during the day while Frank would stand guard at night so there was always someone up.

Sean went to the bedroom he was assigned, across from Aubrey, and set his luggage inside the door. Then he crossed the hall to Aubrey's room.

He paused in the entrance. "After the kids go to bed, I'd like to work on the notebook. You don't have to. This week has been extremely difficult for you."

She twisted around and faced him. "I'm helping. The sooner we find out what's going on, the sooner my children will be back with me in Port Bliss. I know this is the best way to keep them safe, but it's going to be hard for me to walk away from them and my mama on Sunday morning."

He bridged the distance between them and clasped her hand. "I know. It wasn't easy for me to leave my family here to take the position in Company D, but I needed to find out what happened to Jack when he'd disappeared. On my downtime I kept looking for him."

"That's why I need to help you. We need to find justice for our loved ones."

The soft look in her eyes tempted him to move even closer. He wanted to take her into his embrace and kiss her. But he didn't want to make things awkward between them. He released her hand and stepped back. "I'll be downstairs in the kitchen. I'm putting on a pot of coffee. Do you need any help with Sammy and Camy?"

"I know it's late, but I'm going to take them swimming so they'll sleep tonight. I'm glad you suggested I have them pack their bathing suits. I don't think they'll be long in the pool. I'll join you after they go to bed."

"I'll take the books you brought and start looking through them."

Aubrey withdrew two from her suitcase and gave them to him. "It's been a while since I went through them."

"See you later." Sean left before he did something like kiss her again. That wouldn't be a good idea.

He made his way to the kitchen, set the books and Samuel's pad on the table, then rummaged through the cabinets until he found the coffee. After he put the pot on, he sat down and stared at the notebook. He hoped Aubrey could figure out what the symbols meant, because right now they looked like chicken scratches.

He picked up the first book and started flipping through the pages, finding a code that was based on lines and dots. He started reading about it, but after a few sentences, the sound of laughter drifted to him. His attention kept being drawn to what was going on in the indoor pool room, not far from the kitchen. He rose and walked into the hallway that led to the pool.

When he entered, Sammy, with his lifejacket on, jumped off the side into the water, making a big splash. Sean laughed. Camy hesitated at the edge, but after Aubrey coaxed her to try, the little girl did. She popped up with the biggest smile on her face. He realized then that in a short time, he'd come to really care about the twins.

"Sean, did you see me jump?" Sammy dog-paddled to the side nearest Sean.

"Yes."

Sammy pointed to his life preserver. "I don't want to wear this. Mama's making me."

Sean neared the boy. "That's because she loves you. Mamas know best." He glanced at Aubrey, who stared at him with a smile on her face. The connection was palpable. He broke eye contact and bent down near Sammy. "Let me see you swim."

Sammy took off across the pool then came back. "See, I can."

"It's a good start, but remember, you don't have to worry about staying above the water because of the life preserver. This way you can relax and go anywhere in the pool, even the deep end."

The young boy glanced around. "It's big." He took off toward the other end of the pool.

Sean sat in a chair and watched the two play while Aubrey exited the pool and threw a large beach towel around herself. After drying off, she slipped on a cover-up, then headed toward him.

"Did you solve the code yet?" She took the seat next to Sean.

"No. But I discovered I need your help."

"I've given the kids a warning. We're leaving in fifteen minutes. Camy wanted to go now. Sammy didn't, so that was my compromise."

Sean saw Sammy yawning. "You may be leaving sooner. He's slowing down."

Not five minutes later, Aubrey's son climbed out of the pool and sat on a lounge chair. Sean ended up carrying the boy upstairs while Aubrey held Camy. Walking down the hallway, he tried to wake up Sammy.

"When he conks out, it's really hard to wake him up.

Camy is the opposite." They entered the kids' bedroom. "Put him on the bed. I'll see to him after I take care of Camy. Thanks for bringing him upstairs."

He laid the child down, glad he wasn't soaking wet, only damp. "See you downstairs."

Then Sean left, pausing at the exit and glancing back. This was what a family felt like. The feelings generated in him made him question his decision not to get too emotionally involved with others. He'd thought that was what made his job easier to perform, but he wasn't so sure that was right anymore.

After a cup of coffee, Aubrey felt sharper and ready to dig into her husband's notebook. "Samuel loved the pigpen cipher example as a secret code, but he would use several different ways to determine the base of the code. That's what we need to discover. Once we do, it will be a matter of translating the signs to letters."

"What made him interested in secret codes?"

"It started when he was a child. Some of the ones he came up with were complex."

"You aren't being very encouraging."

She grinned. "Think positive. I broke a couple of his hard ones. I know how he thought—when it came to codes, not logically, which would make it harder for a computer to break it right away."

"If we don't, I'll have to give it a try on Monday. I really don't want anyone else to know about Samuel's notepad. This may be our chance to find out what happened two years ago. I don't want anything to interfere with that. The cartel is powerful, and we need to remember that at all times."

"Then let's get down to it. I want answers, too." For

the first time in months, she thought she had a chance of discovering who killed Samuel. She took the other book and flipped through the pages until she found the section that discussed pigpen ciphers. "Here's what I'm talking about." She explained it was a substitution code with a symbol, not a letter or number. She drew a tic-tac-toe grid and placed letters in it. "There are a lot of ways you can do this to mix things up. I think we just have to find the right grid and order of letters."

"What were the ones he used? Let's start there."

"There were three major ones I knew about. I'll draw the guide for them, then we need to see if the substituted letters make sense." Aubrey made a key for one and slid it to Sean, then she worked on the second and third sources for the code.

Hours later, after her third cup of coffee when the symbols began to blur together, she stood and stretched, her muscles cramped. "It isn't the three Samuel used a lot in the past. We're going to have to think outside the box."

"Think outside what box?" Claire asked as she came into the kitchen.

"What are you doing down here?" Sean peered at the clock on the wall. "It's five o'clock in the morning. You aren't a morning person."

"That's changed since I was assigned to the day shift at the police headquarters. Now Thomas and I both work on the same shift." His sister stood at the end of the table. "What are y'all doing, Sean?"

"Trying to figure out a message in code and running into a brick wall—twenty feet high."

Claire chuckled. "I'd say it's time for a long break. Then you might have the energy to leap over that barrier."

"I'm not sure that's possible." Aubrey gathered the papers into a stack. "But it's good advice. Sometimes thinking about something for a long time can actually hamper us. Let's get some sleep and work on this later today."

Sean picked up the books. "Good suggestion, sis. I'll try. See you later today."

As Aubrey mounted the stairs, she kept thinking she was missing something. But no matter how hard she tried to figure out what that could be, she came up blank. "I definitely need a break. I just hope I can sleep, or I'm going to be worthless." She stopped at the door into her bedroom and turned toward Sean behind her. "Surely two brilliant minds like ours can break this code," she said with a chuckle.

"We will. It's time to close the cold cases. This may be the key to your husband's murder."

The best decision she'd made last week was calling Sean for help with her situation. This past week could have gone much worse if she hadn't. "Thank you for coming to my rescue last Friday." She stood on tiptoes and was only going to give him a peck on the cheek for his help. At the last second, she turned slightly and kissed him on the lips. Again, her intention was for a brief connection, but his arms went around her, and he held her closer while deepening the kiss. She relished every second in his embrace.

He finally leaned back, his eyes smoky. "See you later."

"Good night."

He swung around and backpedaled. "Don't you mean good morning? The sun will be up in an hour."

She grinned and quickly went into her bedroom

before she did something else foolish. What was she thinking when she kissed him?

When she caught sight of her bed, the exhaustion she'd held at bay swamped her all at once. She moved to it and collapsed onto it. Weariness won out, and sleep descended...

"Mama. Mama. Get up. I want to go swimming again."

Aubrey slowly opened her eyes to find Sammy's face only inches from hers. What time was it? She rolled her head toward the window. Dim light streamed through the gaps.

"It's a little early to swim."

Sammy lifted his arm and plopped a toy car on the bed beside Aubrey. "It's backward." He stuck out his lower lip. "Won't work."

She sat up. "Honey, wheels roll both ways. You know tha—"

*That's it! I think I can solve the code.*

She hoped anyway.

# NINE

In the den, the sunlight streaked a path toward the game table where Sean sat, trying to figure out the code. He used a technique he did when he solved cipher quotes in the newspaper. He looked at frequent patterns of letters. All single letters were either an *a* or *i*. He thought he discovered the word *the*. He took a page he'd written out and started filling in those letters above the symbol to see what he came up with.

The door opened. He looked up. Aubrey scurried into the room with a big grin on her face. "I figured out how to solve the code."

"How?"

She took the chair next to him. "Once Samuel reversed the alphabet on top of starting in a different place." She drew the first grid and started with the letter *r*. "He still used the pattern of dots and lines as he always did but in a different order. Then he went backward. In the first tic-tac-toe grid it starts with *r*, then *q*, *p*, *o*, *n*, *m*, *l*, *k* and *j*. Then you do the next grid starting with *i* and repeat the process."

Sean set aside the sheet he'd been working on and started fitting the letters into the grids Samuel used. "Did you get any sleep?"

"Three hours, until Sammy came into my bedroom and woke me up. He wanted to go swimming. But he said something that triggered a memory."

"If this works, I'll take him swimming anytime he wants."

She laughed. "Don't say that to him. He'll wake you up in the middle of the night." She looked at him. "How about you? It looks like you've been down here for a while."

"A couple of hours. If we solve it, I'll crash later." When he finished plugging in the letters and put dots where Samuel used to, he pulled over the sheet he'd been working on.

"You've already got some letters over the symbols."

"Instead of doing crossword puzzles, I used to decipher coded quotes by famous people in the newspaper." Sean began putting letters down on the sheet. "It looks like this might be it."

"Your *the* fits where this one does."

When he'd decoded the first paragraph, he slanted a glance at Aubrey. Her face paled as she stared at the words her husband had written.

"'If you are reading this, that means I am dead. I was working with Jack McNair, who has been missing for the past two days. I am sure he is dead,'" Sean read, then lifted his gaze to link with hers.

"We have a lot of work to do. I can help you for a little while, but once Sammy and Camy finish their breakfast, I promised I would take them swimming again. If they had their way, they would turn into raisins."

"We have time. We can work, then take them swimming. We'll be able to finish this today. There's not a lot I can do from here anyway. When we go back to Port Bliss tomorrow, I'll dive into anything that your husband had concerns about." Sean turned the page in the notebook. "You take the left side and decode it. I'll do the one on the right."

Sean started writing the letters down. As he worked, myriad emotions flittered through him, from surprise to sadness to anger. According to what Samuel had written, Jack had been caught up in the cartel by accident. His roommate began working for the cartel and witnessed some of the transactions. His younger brother had never said anything about having a roommate.

The door flew open and both Camy and Sammy, wearing their swimsuits, ran into the den. "We're ready," they said at the same time.

Sean and Aubrey looked at each other and laughed.

Wearing her life jacket, Camy took Aubrey's hand and pulled on it. "C'mon, Mama."

Sammy did the same to Sean, tugging him out of his seat.

"We don't have our swimsuits on."

"Okay." Sammy continued dragging Sean forward into the hallway and toward the stairs.

At the bottom of the steps, Sean stopped and held his ground while Aubrey's son kept trying to budge him. "Are you finished, buddy?"

Sammy nodded and dropped Sean's hand.

He scooped the little boy up into his arms and mounted the staircase. On the second floor, he put Sammy down. "While I'm getting changed, you need your life jacket."

He ran by Aubrey into his room. "Be right back."

She approached Sean. "Has anyone told you that you would make a good father?"

He'd let his little brother down. He'd let his father down. He hadn't been able to protect Jack in the end. "Does my older sister count?"

"Of course. I'm looking forward to meeting her this afternoon. I wish her children were coming, too."

"They're five, seven and nine and don't know how to keep a secret. At least Ella can."

As Sammy came flying out of his bedroom with his vest on, Aubrey moved in front of Sean. "Slow down. The pool isn't going anywhere. We're going to change while you go downstairs and sit on the bottom step with Camy."

Sammy hurried toward the steps.

"Slowly, young man." Aubrey shook her head as she walked to her bedroom and Sean escaped into his. In the past he'd wanted a family, but his wife hadn't. Then Jack got caught up with the wrong people, and no matter what he'd said to his little brother, it didn't change anything. Instead, they argued, and finally Jack had left Amarillo and moved to the Port Bliss area.

As long as Jack had been missing, he'd hoped that his brother would change and that Sean could mend the rift between them. But now that he was dead, that wasn't possible.

His track record wasn't stellar.

Maybe if he found his brother's killer, he could move on. At the moment, his only hope was hidden in Samuel's notebook. But after two years, the case was cold and more difficult to solve than ever.

* * *

Sunday morning, an hour before Sean and Aubrey would be leaving, her mother insisted everyone at the house sit down to a big breakfast in the dining room. As soon as Camy and Sammy had stuffed their pancakes into their mouths, they wanted to go swimming.

Texas Ranger Pierce Claiborne came into the room after making his rounds and said, "I can take y'all if it's okay with your mother."

Aubrey breathed a sigh of relief. If her twins were enjoying the pool, she and Sean might be able to slip away without a lot of dramatics from them. "That would be great. They have to wear their life preservers, though."

Sammy jumped to his feet, followed by Camy, and they rushed toward the staircase.

Claire and Thomas looked at each other then stood. "We'll be waiting outside to take you to the airport."

Her mama gathered the dishes and stacked them on the tray she'd used to bring them into the dining room. "I'm going to start cleaning up." She came around and hugged Aubrey. "We'll be all right. Please take care of yourself."

Emotions jammed Aubrey's throat. In response, she nodded.

After her mama left, Pierce sat in a chair across from her and Sean. "I have some news from Port Bliss. Early this morning, there was a fire at the jail where Villa is. It was put out quickly and no prisoners were hurt badly. A few had smoke inhalation problems, along with one guard, but otherwise the fast action of a couple of the deputies on duty prevented it from being a much worse situation. They are considering moving Villa to the holding cell at the courthouse and adding extra guards from the US Marshals' office."

"Thanks for letting us know. It shouldn't delay the trial tomorrow." Hopefully what was going on in Port Bliss would end when she was no longer attached to Villa. She would especially be glad when the main witness testified.

"I appreciate the update." Sean shook his head. "Another attempt at interrupting the trial. Law enforcement officers have been stretched thin since all this began. Whoever is behind this is getting desperate."

Pierce rose. "That might be to your advantage in the long run. Desperation can lead to mistakes."

"That's what I'm counting on." Sean rose and shook his friend's hand. "I hear the kids coming down the stairs. We'll say goodbye in here, then you can take them swimming."

"We're ready," Sammy announced in a loud voice as he came to a halt in the dining room.

"Yeah!" Camy said right next to her brother.

Aubrey loved seeing her children with huge smiles on their faces. She'd realized in the past day that the twins loved swimming. One of the memories she wouldn't forget was when Sean started teaching both of them how to swim. Sammy even went across the pool without a life preserver, while Camy swam a couple of yards before clinging to Sean.

Aubrey stopped in front of her children. "Sean and I are leaving, but we'll see you soon. *Abuela* thought it would be fun to go on a little mini vacation. You both need to do what she says, and listen to the other adults, as well."

Sammy vigorously nodded his head.

Camy frowned, tears shining in her eyes. "Why can't you stay?"

"I have to go to work tomorrow. But after this trial, I plan on taking you on another vacation to the beach, so practice your swimming."

Sammy put his arm around Camy. "We'll be okay."

The knot in Aubrey's throat swelled. She hugged Camy, then Sammy. "I'll call you every night."

Aubrey watched her children take Pierce's hand and leave. Tears blurred her vision. When they disappeared from view, she dipped her head and stared at the floor where they had been a few seconds before. One tear fell from her eye.

Sean put his arm around her and pressed her against his side. "Samuel's notebook has given me a couple of leads. Two years ago, there was a mole in the police department in Port Bliss. I should be able to get a list of who was employed. It's a start. Samuel had a few suspicions, which might help me narrow down the identity of the mole. That's what I'll be working on when we get back."

"But it's been two years. That person may be long gone."

"That's possible, but the cartel would most likely put pressure on the mole to stay. I'll check on anyone who's left, too. Let's go. The plane will be landing in fifteen minutes."

Aubrey started walking toward the entry hall where their luggage was. "It was nice to get away from Port Bliss."

Sean heaved both suitcases and stepped outside first. Thomas had pulled the car up to the front of the house.

After Sean set the bags on the ground by the rear side fender, he opened the door for Aubrey and whispered into her ear, "This mole was behind my brother's death. I have more than one reason to find him. I won't rest until I figure out who it is."

"Then we'll have some closure on Samuel and Jack's murders. The mole might not be the henchman who killed them, but he was behind it—that and the cartel lieutenant in this area. Too bad it wasn't Villa. He didn't come to Port Bliss until about twenty months ago." The one before him had disappeared. "Was the prior lieutenant one of the bodies found at the burial grounds?"

"Maybe. They're still trying to ID them." Sean waited until Aubrey climbed into the back seat, then he put the suitcases in the trunk and slid into the car next to her.

Aubrey reclined back against the seat and closed her eyes. Her husband's last comment in the notebook was that he was afraid more than one law enforcement officer might be involved. Was that why Samuel had felt he had to keep this all secret—even from her?

After escorting Aubrey to the courthouse Monday morning, Sean crossed the street to talk with Juan Perez, who had a list of employees who worked for the police when Samuel was murdered.

This wasn't going to be an easy conversation with the police chief, who had been hired eighteen months ago when the last one retired and moved to Tulsa, Oklahoma, where his son and family now lived. Juan couldn't be the mole that Samuel referred to in his notebook because he'd come from Fort Worth after Samuel was killed. Sean had a good working relationship with

Juan, but what if he had become recruited by the cartel as a mole, too, after he arrived? It was even possible the retired police chief had been working for the cartel and had been the one who killed Samuel.

As he entered the police station, Sean remembered how the last drug raid he participated in nearly two weeks ago failed when it shouldn't have. He'd thought someone had tipped off the people in the operation. Since Sean had only worked with the Port Bliss Police on the raid, that meant the informer was possibly someone in this building. The mole could lead Sean to the killer of Samuel and Jack. But also, the cartel spy could be responsible for what was happening now with the current trial and Aubrey. He would investigate the former police chief, but he didn't think it was him.

Sergeant Vic Daniels approached Sean. "We finally think we've found the white car with the partial license number you wanted. A couple, Mr. and Mrs. Kirkland, returned from visiting their family and discovered it in their driveway. It doesn't belong to them. They have no idea where it came from."

"Where is it now?"

"Still at their house. They live outside town on a few acres off Bayshore Drive."

"Write their name and address down, and I'll pick it up after I talk with Chief Perez."

"Will do."

Sean continued his trek to Juan's office, where his secretary waved him through. Sean knocked once, then opened the door. The police chief sat at his desk, staring at a paper before him. He lifted his head, his expression sober.

"Another missing case has been solved. Paul Davis,

one of the older bodies at the burial ground, has been ID'd with dental records. Your brother reported him missing about six months before Jack disappeared."

Sean slipped into the chair in front of Juan's desk. "Do you have the missing-person report on Davis?"

"Yes." The police chief passed the folder to Sean.

He scanned it. "He was my brother's roommate."

"At the time Davis disappeared, Jack was on the oil rig. We didn't take it too seriously, because Davis had moved around several times. Jack insisted he would have let him know. When your brother returned to the apartment, it was a mess. Again, he said that wasn't like Davis. That he was a neat freak."

"Why didn't you tell me about this guy?"

"Because I'm just finding out about the Davis missing-person case. I wasn't here at the time it happened. I was still in Fort Worth. The only reason I know now is because he was one of the bodies found."

"Who worked on the case?"

"Officer Cal Adams answered the call from your brother. Later Sergeant Daniels took over investigating the missing-person case. His notes are in this file. Jack never said anything to you about a roommate?"

Sean shook his head. "My brother and I weren't on great speaking terms."

"I'm sorry about that."

"So it looks like Paul Davis was probably murdered by the cartel, like my brother."

"Either that or it was a huge coincidence that the male nurse was buried close to a place where others were disposed." Juan closed the folder and pushed it to the side. "I've got the list you requested. What are you looking for?"

"Information from a reliable source has surfaced that there's a mole in your police department."

Juan frowned. "That's what I was thinking, and one of the reasons I'm here working in Port Bliss. I thought it was Officer Adams. Now I'm not so sure."

"Why?"

"I went to talk to him this weekend before he left the hospital. He couldn't think of anyone who would shoot at him. I went by his house yesterday after he was released from the hospital. He answered the door and came out onto the porch to talk to me."

"How was he?"

Juan tilted his head to the side and thought for a few seconds. "I'd say scared. I guess that's the best word to use. I asked him if he wanted protection. He didn't."

"Where was his wife?" Sean remembered meeting Jana at last year's Fourth of July picnic.

"I don't know. After a few minutes, he said he was tired and needed to go inside and lie down. In other words, his message to me was to get lost. I plan to go back later today."

"I think I should pay him a visit when I leave here, if that's okay with you."

"Yes. He might talk to you." Juan passed him a piece of paper. "This is the list you wanted. Most of the officers I have were here then. Officers Johnston and Watkins joined us this past year."

"Thanks. The trial should wrap up in a couple days."

"Not looking forward to tomorrow, with the star witness testifying."

"Yeah, Aubrey told me she might be finished early today. They start with Mrs. Fields's testimonial tomorrow. Then the defense has to present their case."

"And we'll all be happy when it's over and life can go back to normal."

Sean rose. "In your dreams."

The police chief chuckled. "We can always wish."

"I'm going to see the white car that I asked Sergeant Daniels to find, then I'll go by Adams's house."

Sean left the police station, crossed the street to the courthouse and walked around the west side of the building to the rear parking lot. When he reached his SUV and slid into the vehicle, he took his phone out and texted Aubrey where he was going and that he would still be back in time for lunch with her in her chambers. He drove to the place on Bayshore Drive and found a white car, as he'd seen on the video footage, parked in the driveway on the right side. He pulled up behind it and headed for the front entrance.

A woman in her sixties with salt-and-pepper hair opened the door before he had a chance to push the doorbell.

"Ma'am, I'm Texas Ranger McNair." He showed her his badge. "I'm here because you reported that the car in your driveway isn't yours. Is that right?"

She nodded. "My husband and I returned from a long, exhausting trip late last night. We were surprised to find that car in our driveway." She waved toward the vehicle. "We were so tired that I decided to report it this morning. I don't think I could have stayed up long enough to talk to any police officer who would come to check on it, so I waited."

"You have no idea whose car this is?"

"No. I don't understand why someone would even park it there. My husband at first thought the owner was in our house, but he let Willie inside to see if some-one was there."

Sean peered over the woman's shoulder and glimpsed a large German shepherd right behind her in the entry hall. "Your dog is Willie?"

"Yes," she answered at the same time the canine barked. She turned toward her pet and said, "Stay," then came out onto the porch. "He's the best watch-dog around. He goes with us when we travel, and no one bothers us." Mrs. Kirkland descended the steps and walked toward the white car. "Why in the world is a Texas Ranger here about this car? It was probably a bunch of kids joyriding."

"The person driving it was possibly involved in a case I'm working. You don't have any idea where it came from? Maybe it was parked in the wrong drive-way. Do any of your neighbors have a car like this?" Sean pointed to the vehicle, noting the damaged rear fender on the driver's side that he'd seen in the surveil-lance cam footage. When he stepped behind the sedan, he took a photo of the license plate, then sent it to Juan to find out who owned the car.

"No one I know. Will you be able to have it removed from our driveway? It's blocking my car in the garage."

"Yes, I'll have it towed away." He handed her his business card. "If you find out anything about how it might have ended up here, please let me know." Sean moved to the driver's-side front door and opened it. He put on gloves then checked for a set of keys to the car. "No keys in it." He shut the door and turned toward Mrs. Kirkland. "Have you or your husband touched this vehicle, especially inside by the driver's seat?"

"I opened the driver's door to see if the keys were

in the ignition so I could move it. I need to go to the grocery store."

"I'd like to take your fingerprints. When we check for latent prints in the car, I want to be able to rule yours out."

She nodded. "I hope you catch who left this car here."

"I hope so, too. I'll be right back. I need to get my kit to take your prints." As he headed for his SUV, he called Juan about having the vehicle towed away and the doors and interior checked for latent prints. He also requested that police officers go house to house to see if anyone in the neighborhood saw the car being left in the driveway.

By the time Sean left the Kirklands' property, the white sedan was being towed away, and he had Mrs. Kirkland's fingerprints. In his SUV, he glanced at the clock and realized he wouldn't have enough time to go by Cal's place. He would go see the police officer after lunch with Aubrey. He hoped Cal might have remembered something about the time he was shot and about Jack's roommate's case. For both his brother and Davis to be killed, probably by the same killer, six months apart, wasn't a coincidence. Did this have anything to do with Jack working undercover for Samuel?

Aubrey dismissed the court. She rose and headed to her chamber, eager for the thick, juicy cheeseburger and vanilla milkshake she'd asked Sean to bring for lunch. When she opened the door to her office, he stood and covered the distance between them.

He clasped her upper arms. "How's it going?"

His question and presence released the tension she'd

held since the trial started this morning. "The prosecutor's main witness is a sixty-year-old woman who saw Bento Villa grab a gun from one of his men and shoot the victim."

"Where was she when the crime went down?"

"On the beach where the body was buried in the sand."

"Which beach?"

"The one off Bayshore Drive."

Sean let go of her arms and took a couple of steps back. "That's what I thought. Bayshore Drive is where the white car trailing you was left in an older couple's driveway. That's where I just came from. And it's not that far from where the burial ground was found. A coincidence that all of this is happening in the same area?"

Aubrey shook her head. "Do you think the person in the white car was the one who killed those people and buried them in the same area?"

"It's looking like that's a possibility."

"So everything comes back to the cartel."

Sean took her hand and tugged her toward the coffee table in front of the couch where he'd laid out their food. "Tell you what. Let's enjoy our lunch. I'm hungry."

"Is that your way of saying let's talk about something else?"

"You know me well."

Yes, she was getting to know him. They'd been thrust together because of this case and trial, but when she was with him, she felt safe even at her own home and now at the safe house with two other Texas Rangers who had worked with Samuel. She and Sean had spent hours on what was happening now and two years ago in Port Bliss, but they'd also spent time sharing who they were beyond a judge and law enforcement officer.

Sean dug into the sack and pulled out her cheeseburger then his. "How were the kids this morning when you talked with them?"

"Missing me—and you—but they're having fun swimming. Pierce has taken them under his wing and is giving them lessons. Apparently, he knows exactly what a four-year-old wants to do."

"Because he has a son who was four once. How's your mother doing?"

"Mama says she feels like she's on vacation. Pierce does so much of what she usually does."

"I've known Pierce a long time. He's a good guy, and I couldn't have asked for a better man to protect your kids and your mother. I miss them."

"So do I," Aubrey murmured right before taking a big bite of her cheeseburger. "Mmm. This is so good. I didn't eat much breakfast. I should have asked you to bring me two of them."

He chuckled. "I actually did. I thought we could split it."

"Sounds great."

For the next ten minutes they both sat and ate their lunch. She felt no need to fill the silence with talking. The quiet and relaxation in her chambers was just what she needed—not to mention having Sean sitting next to her, enjoying his food and occasionally smiling at her.

After he cut the third cheeseburger in half, she leaned back against the couch, exhaling slowly. "I wish we could stay in here all afternoon."

"How's the testimony going?"

"Slow. The defense is challenging everything they can. After lunch they have their chance with Mrs. Fields."

"Where was she when she witnessed the killing?"

"Behind a dune. She has a spot where she sunbathes and can't be seen by people walking along the beach. Weather permitting, she does it every day for half an hour. Her way of getting her vitamin D, she says. When she heard the voices, she peeked over the top of the dune with sea grass and caught Villa shooting Hector Martin. Her life has been so disrupted. I know the feeling."

"This afternoon I'm only going to see Cal Adams."

"How's he doing?" Aubrey reclined back and finished the last bite of her cheeseburger.

"He didn't want to talk to the police chief yesterday. It might be depression. I've seen that happen when a law enforcement officer is shot—actually anyone. But I'm going to see him because he was the one who handled my brother's roommate disappearing six months before Jack. Cal was first on the scene. Sergeant Daniels took over the case to investigate the missing person. I also found out that another body from the burial ground was identified. It was Paul Davis, the roommate. Jack came back from working on the oil rig to find Paul gone, but not his stuff. My brother reported him missing."

"Why didn't you know this?"

"The police chief didn't even know it. It happened before he came to Port Bliss and was named the police chief."

"What do you think Cal can tell you?"

"Probably nothing. But he interviewed Jack right

after it happened. I want to know what my brother said to him. His impressions of the case. I've read the sergeant's notes on it, and there wasn't much there. Lots of dead ends."

"I hope you can get answers."

"I want closure on my brother's murder just as you do for Samuel." He placed his hand over hers. "We'll get justice. Jack made a lot of mistakes. I think he decided to help your husband when Paul disappeared. I wish Jack had a notebook like Samuel, with evidence I can follow."

"I know. At least we found Samuel's notes and his concerns about a cartel mole at the police department."

"I had my suspicions when my last drug raid fell apart. Nothing makes me angrier than a corrupt law enforcement officer. Most of them aren't, but the ones that are dirty hurt the rest of us."

Aubrey put her hands on the couch and shoved herself to her feet. "I can't wait until this testimony is over. From the list of defense witnesses, we should be able to send the jury to deliberation on Wednesday. Maybe I'll get my life back by this weekend."

Sean stood, smiling down at her. "I hope so. When does the trial start this afternoon?"

Aubrey checked her watch. "In five minutes. Our time has flown by. We should be wrapped up today by five."

"Good. That'll be enough time for me to talk with Cal. I'll be back before that." He cupped her face, his soft blue eyes transfixed on her. He dipped his head and brushed his mouth across hers. "I'll do everything I can to protect you."

After he left her office, Aubrey stared at the door into the corridor. She touched her lips where she still felt his kiss. She was falling for him, but she could never go through what happened to Samuel again. She needed this over with so she could put some distance between them.

Sean hated leaving Aubrey, but the security at the courthouse had been tightened. The rest was in the Lord's hands. He quickly made his way down to the first floor and out the rear exit with two deputy sheriffs at the door checking everyone coming into the building, scanning them and their belongings. In the parking lot, an extra law enforcement officer from the US Marshal's office stood guard near the vehicles they had used bringing the star witness to Villa's trial.

Fifteen minutes later, Sean arrived at Cal's house and strode toward it. He rang the doorbell, then knocked when he received no answer. He walked around the place to see if there was a window he could look inside. His gut tightened when he came back to the front. Something didn't feel right. He looked at the garage, but there was no way he could see if Cal's car was in there.

He walked back to his SUV and sat out front, trying to decide what to do. Leave or try to get in the house? His cell phone rang, a number he didn't recognize, and he answered it.

"Sean, this is Cal. I'm inside my home, but if I open the door and let you in, they will kill my wife."

"Who is they?"

"I don't know. I need you to drive away. Please."

"Okay." Sean started the SUV and pulled away from the curb. "But if you're in trouble, I don't want to go far. Tell me what's going on. Do you know who shot you? And why?"

"I don't know who did, but I think I know why."

Sean parked a couple of streets away to continue the conversation. He scanned the area, looking for anyone who might have followed him from Cal's.

"I overheard two people talking about the cartel, one a police officer."

"Which officer?"

"I don't know. The man was talking to an officer on a phone. I only overheard one side of it, but it was clear what they were discussing—Villa's trial and how to stop it. I've been trying to figure out who the police officer was, but I haven't been able to."

"Did you see what this other man looked like?"

"Yes—at the time I didn't know him. But when the drawing of the person who posed as the nurse at the hospital came out, I discovered he was my wife's cousin from Houston. I knew she was worried about something, and she finally said something to me right before I came over to the judge's house to stand guard that night I was shot. She hadn't seen her cousin in several years and was surprised to discover he was the impostor at the hospital. I told her not to say anything and I would take care of the problem. At first, I was going to go to the police chief, but after wrestling with the issue, I decided to talk to you that Friday morning first."

"So where is your wife?"

"I don't know, but when I came home from the hospital, I knew there had been a struggle in our bedroom. Soon after I arrived, I received a call from Jana, begging me not to tell anyone about her cousin. Then he came on the phone and told me what would happen to her and me if I did. I know they're watching my house. It might even be bugged."

"Then why did you call me?"

"I'm in the shower with the water running."

Sean rubbed his hand against his chin, trying to figure out what to do. He wanted to go to Juan, but maybe that wasn't the best idea with the mole still unknown. He hated questioning Juan's integrity, but people's lives were at stake. "Do you have any idea who the police department mole is?"

"No."

"Then I have to find your wife's cousin. He knows. What's his name?"

"Mario Bravo. Jana confessed to me she was afraid of him. I don't think he'll tell you anything. I've never heard such fear in my wife's voice."

But at least he would be able to bring in his brother's killer and possibly even Samuel's, even if he didn't get anything from Bravo. "Any ideas where I should look for him?"

"This is a long shot, but when he was here a couple of years ago, I met him briefly. I overheard Jana talking to him. He stayed at a house near the sand dunes. Jana mentioned it belonged to her family."

"But you don't know exactly where?"

"No. But look at the property records at the courthouse. I need to hang up, or whoever put the bugs in my house will know something is up."

"When I have answers, I'll be showing up at your house."

Sean disconnected the phone call, made a U-turn and headed back toward the courthouse. He had to find Bravo and Cal's wife. The man—most likely the cleaner—wouldn't think twice about killing his cousin, and Sean wouldn't allow him to add another person to the list of people he'd murdered.

When he arrived at the courthouse, he hurried inside and to the records department on the first floor at the front of the building. Time was of the essence. After having seen the work of the cleaner firsthand, he didn't doubt Jana's life was at stake, even if the killer was her cousin.

He'd been here before and knew the clerk behind the counter. He approached Betty, who had been in the records department for thirty-five years. "I need to know if there is any property in Port Bliss owned by the Bravo family."

"Anything for you. Is this about a case?"

"You know I can't tell you anything, Betty." He winked at her.

She laughed while she went to her desk and sat at her computer. He came around the counter and stood by her. While he waited, several others entered the office, and Betty's assistant helped the first one.

He kept his eye on the people around him while Betty searched. Time dragged by. The door opened again, and a woman with a toddler positioned herself at the end of the small line forming.

"I've got something," Betty said.

As Sean looked down at the computer, a loud boom shook the building, and all the lights went out. The screen went black.

# TEN

Aubrey sat in her courtroom, watching the jury's faces as the defense asked yet another question about Mrs. Fields's eyesight. She was about to tell Villa's lawyer to move on when a loud sound reverberated through the room while it rocked. The glass in two windows toward the front where she presided over the trial blew out.

A bomb?

Two deputy sheriffs assigned to this court closed in on her from each side. All she could think about was that one or both of them could be a mole like Samuel talked about in his notebook. They had no idea who it was and if it extended into the sheriff's department.

The overhead lights flickered off.

Everyone rallied from their dazed state and began a charge for the double doors. Several US Marshals took Mrs. Fields under their care while one of them got on his mic, probably trying to figure out what was happening. The sheriff's detail surrounded Villa.

"Judge, you need to leave here now," Deputy Simpson said.

His words drew her attention back to the two officers, one on each side of her. She rose.

Deputy Worth was in the lead as they moved to the door that connected the hallway to her chambers. She glanced back at the people still trying to exit the courtroom. "What are we going to do?"

"Our job. Get you to a safe place," Simpson said behind her. "It'll be less crowded going out of your office."

Where was Sean? She wished he was here. As she entered her chambers, Simpson was on his radio, trying to find out which way would be better to leave the building. The nearest exit was the front.

After he turned off the radio, he opened the door. "The rear exit isn't as crowded. I'll take the lead. Worth, you follow."

While she and the two deputies headed toward the stairs to the first floor, she peered back at the crowd trying to go down the large, wide staircase that went all the way to the third level. At the moment it was crammed with people trying to get out of the building.

Simpson turned left, then right and walked down the corridor to the end, where steps led to the bottom floor. Aubrey and the two officers melted into the flow of the few others making their way to a door that opened not far from the rear exit.

Simpson worked his way to the front and held up his hand for everybody to wait while he cracked the door open. The sound of rapid-fire gunshots resonated through the air. The deputy sheriff slammed the door shut. "We can't get out this way. Back up the stairs."

Aubrey spun around on the third step and followed Deputy Worth upward. Her heart thumped against her chest. As he reached for the knob on the second floor, another burst of bullets blasted the hallway on this level.

They were trapped!

\* \* \*

What light remained in the records office came through the one window facing the front of the courthouse. Sean hurried around the counter as people started for the door. "Let me check the lobby first." He forged his way through the staff and customers who had been standing in line.

He eased the door open. The lights were off in the lobby, but with the large double front doors and floor-to-ceiling windows on each side of them, everything seemed all right—except for a flood of bodies racing toward the exit in their panic, some shoving others out of the way.

He turned from the entrance and said, "People are panicking. You need to hurry. This office is close to the exit, and only a handful are at the door right now."

Sean stood to the side, glimpsing the chaos descending on the lobby as the customers and staff of the records office dived into the mob. He made a call to Sheriff Bailey to report the situation, then left the records office last, going in the opposite direction, trying to stay on the edge of the throng. He needed to make sure Aubrey got out of the building all right. After glancing at the main staircase jammed with people, he decided to use the set of steps Aubrey usually took to get to her office from the rear entrance. As he neared the corridor that led to the back, the sound of gunfire riddled the air.

Several people ran toward him, fear stamped on their faces. One passed him, then pointed in the direction he'd come from. "Men with guns are coming into the building."

Behind Sean, more gunshots went off across the

lobby. He turned toward the noise. The somewhat orderly crowd became a frightened mob with one goal—get out of the building. The shooters, dressed all in black with masks over their faces, released a barrage of gunfire over the heads of the people still on the main staircase, as though the goal was to cause a stampede. A few jumped over the railing in order to get away. The rest fled as fast as they could.

"Get into a room with a window, lock the door and try to get out that way." Sean removed his weapon from his holster, intending to take as many gunmen out as he could without endangering innocents. He positioned himself behind a column and aimed at a man all in black rushing toward the stairs, waving his gun at the crowd as though he was saying, "Get out of my way or I'll shoot."

But every time he had a chance to fire his gun, a civilian was in the way. The men in black made their way to the stairs. The steps were clearing, but not the people between Sean and the staircase. The invaders used the crowd as a shield and disappeared from his view. Sean rushed after them as backup waded through the crowd toward him. A spurt of gunfire sounded above him, coming from the east, then a barrage of bullets came from the west.

They were going after Villa, and Sean needed to stop them and find Aubrey. He headed up to the second floor with four deputy sheriffs right behind him. Although he didn't think anyone was in Aubrey's courtroom, he had to check. No guards stood at the double doors into the room. He reached the entrance and opened it. Empty. He quickly assessed the place—windows blown out, no bullet holes visible and no blood.

As he turned away from the double doors, the four deputies approached. The escape plan the US Marshals had developed was the stairs on the west side of the building and out the third door, while Aubrey would leave through her office and use the steps on the east side to go out the rear door to the parking lot.

Sean pointed to one of the deputies. "You come with me. The rest of you go to the west stairs. The marshals may need your help."

As he and Deputy Garcia ran toward the hallway that led to the east exit, Sean prayed Aubrey was unhurt. Both Simpson and Worth were dedicated to their job. But as he turned the corner, a doubt niggled at his mind. What if one of them was working for the cartel?

Aubrey's breaths came out in short gasps, her heart beating so rapidly that she felt a little light-headed. The door below them slammed shut while they were coming up the stairs.

Simpson pointed upward, then started up the steps to the top level. Worth took up the rear. The sound of footfalls heightened the urgency to get out of the stairwell.

As they neared the third floor, sweat rolled down her face. She stumbled on a step and nearly went down. Worth caught her and steadied her, helping her up the last few stairs and through the doorway into a deserted hallway.

Aubrey leaned against the wall, catching her breath while Simpson grabbed a fire ax and blocked the door from opening. Worth went to the end of the corridor to check out the situation. He waved for her and Simpson to come to him.

Worth looked left then right. "This floor is deserted. We need to find a room to hole up in and call for backup. I'm sure by now more help has arrived. Hopefully the building will be secured soon."

As the two deputies searched for the best place to wait for help, all Aubrey could think of was what had caused the explosion. A bomb? Could there be another?

Sean sneaked up to where two corridors intersected. He'd heard shots coming from this direction. He peeked around the corner. The area in front of the east staircase was deserted. He signaled to Deputy Garcia to check the offices on the left while he did the ones on the right. No one was inside any room, including Aubrey's.

When they reached the door to the stairwell, Sean went first. He leaned over the banister and scanned the first-floor area he could see. Nothing. Then he looked upward and didn't see anything there, either. In the distance he heard gunfire, but nothing close by. He hoped the backup was able to catch all of the members of the assault team on the courthouse. He started down the stairs to the bottom level. When he pushed the door open, he peered out into the hallway and noticed a couple of the raiding party were shot and down on the ground, as were two deputy sheriffs.

"Make sure they're secure," Sean said and waved toward the assailants while he went to check the officers.

Deputy Lockhart groaned and struggled to get up, blood running down his arm.

"Stay still. I'll call for help." Sean knelt and felt the pulse on the other deputy sheriff. Nothing.

He quickly called for an ambulance as the sheriff,

along with a couple of deputies, rounded the building and rushed toward them.

Sean stood, glancing toward three members of the assault team down on the floor. Worth had everything under control as Sheriff Bailey pushed through the door, his jawline set in anger, his look dark and intense when his gaze fell onto the prone deputy.

"He's dead." Sean glanced at Lockhart, who sat against the wall, an ashen tint to his face. "Did Judge Madison leave out this door?"

"I don't think so, but I'm not sure. I was hit over the head and passed out for—" Lockhart closed his eyes for a few seconds "—I don't know how long."

"I didn't see her outside, but Simpson called and told me that he, Deputy Worth and the judge were in a room on the third floor. Number 316."

"Are they okay?"

The sheriff nodded. "But that was five minutes ago. I'll take care of this. Go look for her. So far the first floor and part of the second are secured."

"Let them know I'm on the way, but to stay put in case there are still members of the assault team up there." Sean paused. "What caused the explosion?"

"The courthouse's transformer was sabotaged. The fire department is handling it, but they want the building evacuated in case the fire spreads to the structure. Take Deputy Garcia with you."

Sean signaled Garcia to join him, and he entered the stairwell, praying that Aubrey was all right.

Aubrey stood to the side of the window overlooking the front of the courthouse. She no longer heard shots.

From her vantage point, she didn't have any idea where the explosion had come from or what caused it. People left the building and mostly kept going, with a few on-lookers stopping across the street. She'd seen the fire trucks arrive on the other side of this place. From what Deputy Simpson heard from the sheriff, the transformer had exploded. Obviously, all of this had been orchestrated by the cartel. Did it work? Had Villa escaped? Was Mrs. Fields okay? How many were killed or hurt? Was Sean all right?

With each minute that ticked away, her worry amplified. This was a perfect example of why she didn't want to care about Sean. It would just end like it had with Samuel. He would leave one day and never come back.

Simpson's phone rang.

She slanted a look at the two deputies, but Simpson's voice was too low to hear. She turned back toward the window, not wanting to know what was going on. She'd find out soon enough.

"Judge, help is on the way," Simpson finally said as he ended the call.

"How bad is it?"

"Sheriff Bailey didn't say, other than that the situation is now under control."

"Thank You, Lord," she whispered, but she felt drained and empty. She didn't know where she'd get the emotional energy to finish the trial. All she wanted to do was make sure Sean was alive and see her children.

A knock sounded at the door.

She pivoted, holding herself tense, as Worth let in Sean and a deputy sheriff. In relief, she collapsed back against the wall by the window. All she'd been able to do until now was relive waiting to hear about her husband two years ago.

Sean crossed the room to her, a grin leaking through his somber expression. "I'm so glad you're all right."

She needed to respond, but her mind went blank. She'd pictured him dead or wounded and wasn't able to get that image out of her mind. She swallowed the tightness in her throat and tried to force a smile to her lips. Instead tears began to flow from her eyes the closer he came to her.

Sean looked over his shoulder and said to the two deputies, "Sheriff Bailey is downstairs by the rear door. Judge Madison and I will be down in a minute."

They left and quietly closed the door.

Sean shifted his full attention to her. Heat singed her cheeks. She hadn't intended to release the emotions churning her stomach, but she couldn't stop her tears. So much had happened in the past week and a half.

Sean enveloped her in his embrace. "Let it go. A lot has been going down lately. Keeping it inside only makes it worse. Take it from me. I've experienced it. When Jack went missing, I blamed myself for him leaving Amarillo and for putting my brother in danger. I'm realizing today I didn't put Jack in danger, but circumstances that were out of my control did. He had a roommate go missing. That led Jack to your husband. That was Jack's choice to try to figure out what happened to his roommate. We can't control a lot of things, and we shouldn't blame ourselves for those things."

"I wish I could control it—then this wouldn't be happening." She swiped her tears away only to have others replace them.

"Life doesn't work that way. Some people think it

can, but they're only fooling themselves. There will come times when I'll feel I can and will try to. It's called being human."

She leaned against him and closed her eyes, drawing strength from the comfort of his arms around her. She wasn't fighting this alone. Sean was by her side. She'd missed that, but she couldn't become too complacent. When this was over with, she would have to pick up the pieces of her life as she'd done two years ago and move on.

After relishing the safety of his arms for a few minutes, Aubrey pulled back and stared up into his face. "Thanks for being here." She took a step away. "But now we need to go find out what the fallout is from today's raid."

"I wouldn't be surprised the sheriff hasn't sent someone to check on us." Sean moved to the closed door and inched it open. After surveying the hallway, he took her hand and stepped out into the corridor, then headed for the stairwell.

No more sounds of gunshots.

In fact, the emptiness of the third floor unnerved her.

When they reached the first level, the paramedics were working on Bill, lying on the gurney. Aubrey wove her way through the crowd, mostly law enforcement and EMTs, and stopped next to Bill. "What happened? Are you going to be all right?"

"Just a flesh wound on my arm. I'll be fine and back to work in no time."

It looked like more than a flesh wound. "How about the lump on your head?"

Bill winced. "I have to admit it hurts."

"I'll be praying for you and the others."

"Appreciate it," he murmured as the paramedics rolled him out the rear door.

Aubrey scanned the hallway where three victims were covered by a sheet, although she glimpsed black clothing under one of them. A shudder rippled down her body.

She stepped next to Sean, who was talking with Sheriff Bailey. "Is Mrs. Fields all right?"

The sheriff nodded. "She's under heavy security."

"If I want to talk to her, who do I go through?"

Sheriff Bailey tapped his chest. "Me. Call me, and I'll arrange it."

"What happened to Villa?"

"He's safe in a jail cell."

"Good. There can't be a repeat of what happened here today. I understand the transformer exploded."

"It was sabotaged. The fire department has the fire, generated from a small explosion, under control. The transformer has to be replaced."

"This trial needs to end as soon as possible for the safety of everyone involved."

"I see someone I need to talk to. I'll be right back." Sean strode down the hall to talk with Deputy Simpson.

The sheriff moved off to the side, away from others in the area. "I'll look for a safe venue for the last part of the trial. How many days do you need?"

Aubrey thought about what was left. "The prosecution has presented its case. And from what I've seen of the defense's case, it shouldn't last more than a day, then closing arguments. So I'm thinking two, maybe three days, then the jury will have to deliberate, which could be hours or days."

"I'll get back with you as soon as I find something."

"I want a small place that can be locked down, easily defended. I want the location a secret. I know after the first day, people—including the cartel—will know where the trial is taking place, but at least Mrs. Fields will be ushered away and not have a second attempt made on her life because of her testimony. She's already given up so much. I don't want her life to be added to the list."

As Sean rejoined them, Sheriff Bailey nodded.

"I want to get Aubrey to the safe house. Let me know any new details about what happened today." Sean placed his hand at the small of her back and maneuvered them through the people in the hallway.

Outside, the stench of a recent fire filled the air. Sean hurried Aubrey to his SUV and inside it. When he slid behind the steering wheel, he threw her a glance before pulling out of the parking space. In the side mirror she spied the Texas Ranger, assigned to protect her at the safe house, following Sean's vehicle as planned.

"Did you work out the details about the trial with the sheriff?"

"Yes. I was surprised you would be back at the courthouse. Did you get anything from Cal?"

"Yes. The identity of the guy in your hospital room."

Aubrey's jaw dropped. She'd never expected something like that. "Who is he? Have you put a BOLO out on him?"

"No, not yet. I was at the courthouse when the explosion occurred because I was looking up a possible piece of property where the guy might be hiding with Cal's wife."

"His wife is gone? Kidnapped?"

"According to Cal. He hasn't said anything because he's afraid his wife's cousin from Houston will kill her. When he came home from the hospital, there was evidence that there had been a struggle."

"Did she ever go visit him at the hospital?"

"Yes, the first day. I think her cousin is the one who shot him and is using her to keep Cal quiet."

"Do you trust Cal?" After all the things that had occurred recently, she was having a hard time trusting anyone, except for Sean.

"Right before the electricity went out, I saw the address of the piece of property that belonged to Cal's wife's family. Apparently her cousin Mario Bravo was here at the time my brother went missing and Samuel was murdered."

"This guy could be the killer."

Sean pulled into the garage of the safe house, with the Texas Ranger who followed them doing the same. "It's possible he's the cleaner my informant told me about."

The other Texas Ranger exited his car and came around the SUV to the driver's side. Sean rolled down the window. "I'm leaving to follow up on a lead that may answer a lot of questions. I'll keep you informed of what's happening."

Texas Ranger Jorge Conde, one of two who helped Sean to guard Aubrey, leaned in and said, "Don't worry. I can always wake up Brett if I think he's needed."

Sean grinned. "We'll get to kid him about sleeping through all the action in the case."

Texas Ranger Conde tipped the brim of his hat and walked toward the house, waiting for her to exit.

Aubrey looked at Sean and reached for his hand closest to her. The physical connection with him enfolded her in calmness. "If her cousin is the cleaner, he'll kill her and finish what he started with Cal."

"I agree. That's why I have Chief Perez watching Cal's house while I find his wife."

"Just the police chief?"

"Yes. I don't know who else to trust, not after what your husband suspected. I'd rather leave the two Texas Rangers here protecting you. Perez wasn't here when my brother and your husband were killed."

Aubrey put her hand on the door handle. "Be careful…" Her throat closed tight around the rest of the words she wanted to say.

Instead she rushed toward the door into the kitchen, where Texas Ranger Conde stood waiting.

The garage door went up, then down after she entered the house. Now all she could do was pray that Sean would return unharmed. She just couldn't consider the other option.


Sean parked his car off the road behind tall vegetation to hide his SUV, then hiked toward the house in the middle of a grove of trees. He cased it for fifteen minutes, circling around it from a distance. It looked deserted. Maybe this wasn't where Jana Adams was being kept. But he had to check it out, especially because this was his only lead.

Sean drew his gun and crept toward the left side of the place. The curtains were open a few inches. He slowly made his way to the window, high off the ground, while constantly scanning the area around him. There was no vehicle in the vicinity.

He started to peer into the house when his cell phone vibrated in his pocket. He quickly stepped away and answered it. "I can't talk now, Cal."

"I just remembered something. When Jana came to pick me up from work and we discussed her cousin and his likeness to the drawing of the fake nurse, there was a chance that Sergeant Vic Daniels overheard part of the conversation. He came around the corner of the police station."

"Right now, I'm at the house that belongs to your wife's family. I don't know if anyone is here."

"I've got to go. Someone is at my door."

"Call me back after you check who it is."

The connection went dead. Sean stuffed his phone into his pocket and moved back to the window to peek inside. His gaze zoomed in on the bed's coverlet—with blood all over it.

He proceeded to the front door. When he tried the knob, it turned. His gun drawn, he moved inside, his focus totally homed in on his surroundings. As he made his way toward the bedroom where he'd seen the bloody coverlet, he took in the indications that someone had been here recently—a glass on the coffee table, an ashtray filled with cigarette butts, a large sweatshirt hanging over a chair.

When he pushed open the door to the bedroom, he swept through it, checking the closet and any place a person could hide before he turned his full attention on the coverlet. The stench of the blood filled his nostrils. The wetness of the blood indicated that whatever caused this had happened recently.

He quickly checked the rest of the house and then placed a call to Cal. He didn't think he would answer, but he hoped he would call him back. When Cal didn't, Sean left a message then punched in the police chief's number to report the scene of a possible crime. "I won't be here. One of my contacts is in trouble." After giving Juan the location of the house, Sean ended the conversation and took photos of the coverlet and each room, then a swab of the blood that hadn't dried yet. As he left, he also snapped a few pictures of the footprints that weren't his in the dirt outside the house.

The drive to Cal's home on the other side of Port Bliss took fifteen minutes. He parked in the driveway and hastened to the front entrance. He rang the bell and even knocked on the door.

He didn't have a good feeling about this.

He put his gloves on and turned the knob. Like at the house in the woods, the door was unlocked, which meant something was wrong, because Cal kept his house locked. Sean started counterclockwise, clearing each room as he progressed through the place. When he walked down the hall leading to the bedrooms, he stopped at the only closed door in the corridor. Stepping to the side, he gripped the knob and shoved the door open. As he moved into the bathroom, he saw a leg draped over the side of a bathtub. As he went farther into the room, he shifted his attention between the tub and the hallway.

When his gaze fell on Cal, dressed as he'd been the last time Sean saw him, he felt for the police officer's pulse.

# ELEVEN

Aubrey paced the living room at the safe house, wishing she could hold her children. She missed them so much, and she hadn't even been away from them for long.

And now she was worried about Sean. He should be back here by now. He'd called earlier to tell her Cal Adams had been murdered and he'd be away for a couple more hours. They didn't talk long, to keep someone from tracing the call, but his statement left her with so many questions—and concerns.

She glanced around the room, taking in her prison. Since Villa's trial started, she'd felt like a prisoner. She wasn't even sure she'd be able to complete the trial anytime soon. She wanted it over for everyone involved. Many had put their lives on hold because of Villa. Poor Mrs. Fields would have to come back so the defense could question her. That was the law. Would today at the courthouse change the woman's mind?

The sound of the garage door going up sent a ripple of relief—and fear—down Aubrey's spine. She headed for the kitchen. Texas Ranger Jorge Conde was already entering the utility room when Sean came into the house.

"It's about time you arrived," Jorge said with a chuckle. "I was beginning to think the judge was going to wear a path in the carpet." He stepped back into the kitchen.

Sean followed, deep lines of exhaustion carved into his face. "Is everything all right here?"

"Now it is." Jorge turned and left the kitchen.

Sean's gaze latched onto Aubrey's and held it. "I'm sorry I couldn't keep you more informed, but things were happening fast. And I don't want anyone to find this safe house. I had to take extra precautions with all that's going down."

"I want to know everything, because I'm tired of running all the different scenarios through my mind." She started for the living room.

Sean grasped her arm and stopped her. "I'm sorry it took so long. I know this is hard on you, but I'm making progress, albeit slower than I want."

The tension in her body melted, her shoulders sagging.

Sean stepped closer and encircled his arms around her. "This will pass. We'll find out who's doing this."

She closed her eyes, relishing the safety and comfort of his embrace. When she finally leaned back and looked up into his face, she wanted to kiss him. But this wasn't the time or the place. Too much was going on in their lives. She had to halt the growing feelings she had for Sean. She wasn't going to put her family in harm's way ever again, which meant she would be stepping down as a judge after this trial.

She pulled back from him and walked toward the living room. When she sat down, he took a seat in a chair across from the couch. Sean's nearness was hard to resist. It would be so easy to give in to her emotions concerning Sean and be right where she'd been with Samuel, with a man whose job was dangerous.

"As you know, I found Cal murdered in the bathroom at his house. His throat was slit. Either he was surprised, or he knew his killer. He didn't put up much of a struggle. Even with his injury, he would have put up a fight."

"Why was he shot and then later finished off at his house?"

"His wife was kidnapped by the nurse impostor, who happens to be Jana Adams's cousin from Houston. The killer used her to keep Cal quiet. I found out something was going on, and Cal confessed. Using that information about the cousin and the family house, I went to it today. I discovered a coverlet soaked with blood in the bedroom. I think Jana was killed, and her cousin went to Cal's to finish cleaning up the loose ends. The police are canvassing the neighbors to see if anyone had a surveillance camera that might have caught who arrived at Cal's place right before he was killed."

"Where's Jana?"

"Probably already buried or in the car the guy was driving. On a neighbor's video footage, we got a break. A black truck with an enclosed back where a body could be hidden was captured, along with a partial license plate. Juan is running it down. He's the only one working on that. He'll call me with any updates. In the meantime, a BOLO has been put out on Mario Bravo and the description of the black pickup the authorities have. Hopefully we'll get a break."

Aubrey clasped her hands and kept rubbing them

together. "So this Mario Bravo is the cleaner sent here a couple of years ago and now?"

"Yes. Sheriff Bailey is digging into that."

"But no rank and file?"

"Right now, I'm keeping this quiet except for a few people in the Texas Rangers as well as Juan and Don. If Villa is convicted, it'll be a blow to the cartel."

*When? The past couple of weeks have been a nightmare.* "Did Don say anything about finding a place to have the trial tomorrow?"

"Yes, at the sheriff's office. They have a large enough room that can hold the essential people for the trial. The security is normally tight and will be even more so. The building is much smaller than the courthouse and will be easier to protect. He said you want to do it as quickly as possible, so it will start tomorrow at ten. He let the US Marshals who are guarding Mrs. Fields know."

Aubrey blew out a long breath. "Good. When will the courthouse be opened again?"

"Not before Thursday, but it could be even longer than that. The whole building is a crime scene, and it will take them a while to process it."

"I need to get back into the building before the trial for items tied to it."

"Give me a list, and I'll do it and bring it to the sheriff's office." He rose and bridged the distance between them. "I don't know about you, but I'm ready to get some sleep." He held out his hand to her.

She shouldn't take it. Instead she should distance herself from him. But the logical part of her didn't win out. She touched his hand, and his fingers closed around hers. He tugged her to her feet, inches away from him. Her heartbeat increased. Her throat went dry. He tilted her head back, so he could look into her eyes. The warmth of his eyes embraced her and left her feeling cherished.

"We'll get through this and get answers for the murders of my brother and your husband. I won't rest until we do."

"I want answers, but not if it's going to put others in danger. How am I going to be able to live with all this?"

"As long as the murderer is out there, he's a danger to others. Not to mention he's part of the cartel." Sean brushed the back of his hand over her cheek. "We both need rest. Tomorrow will be a big day. C'mon. I'll walk you to your room."

At the door to her bedroom, she twisted around and touched his face. "I don't know what I would have done without you. Thanks for coming that day I called you for help."

"Anytime. Good night." He gave her a smile then backed away, waiting for her to go inside.

She did and locked her door, as well as checked each window with bars over them. She sank onto her bed, missing her children—missing Sean. But soon, she would have to walk away from him when their lives returned to normal. Sammy and Camy deserved that.

After escorting Aubrey to the sheriff's office, Sean met Juan at Cal's home, going through the place to find the bugs that Cal said were there. Yesterday they had processed the crime scene. Sean had sent all the evidence they found to the lab the Texas Rangers used, putting a rush on matching the DNA on the bloody coverlet to the DNA from a hairbrush holding long black hair in the master bedroom. Cal's wife, Jana, had long black hair. If the DNA was the same, then with the amount of blood on the coverlet, it was most likely that Jana Adams was already dead. A cadaver dog had been brought in to check the woods around the house where the coverlet was. The dog didn't find anything.

Sean met Juan in the living room. "I found two bugs. How about you?"

"The same." Juan moved to the front door and left the house.

Sean followed. "Cal was right about the listening devices. Which leaves us with the question of who the mole is for the cartel Samuel was looking for. Cal thought the sketch looked like his wife's cousin. The photo of Mario Bravo had similarities to the drawing of the fake nurse. Not long after Cal voiced his concerns, he was shot at. Was that just a coincidence, or was it what led to his ultimate death?"

Sean's cell phone rang—it was the sheriff. "How's it going with the trial so far?"

Don chuckled. "I knew that would be the first thing you'd ask. Aubrey is fine, and except for a mob of reporters outside the station, everything is going as planned."

"Good. Has Mrs. Fields left yet?"

"No, the defense is still questioning her, trying everything to tear down her testimony, but Mrs. Fields is a sharp lady. The reason I called is to let you know that the black truck has been found on the side of a county road." Don gave Sean the location where the truck was parked. "I can spare two deputies with a dog to search for whoever was driving the truck. With the trial at the sheriff's office, I need to stay here. I thought you might want to go search for the person in the truck."

"We don't know how long the vehicle has been there?"

"No. So it could be any time from when it was caught on the neighbor's security camera at two yesterday afternoon to when it was found just thirty minutes ago by a highway patrol officer."

"I'm leaving Cal's house and will go there. Do you think the guy has fled on foot?" Sean started for his SUV.

"Don't know. That's why I'm sending the dog."

"Let your deputies know I'm on my way. Thanks for telling me." Sean disconnected the call and opened the driver's-side door.

Juan quickened his pace to his squad car. "I'm following you. It would be nice to find Cal's murderer right away."

Juan followed Sean to the location of the black truck. Two other deputy sheriffs' cars were parked behind the pickup that was off the road in the dirt. Sean inspected the unknown vehicle that had been seen on the neighbor's video footage at the time of Cal's death. Then he walked around it, to the rear. Behind the pickup were single tire tracks, like a motorcycle would make. Maybe he had the bike in the back of his truck bed. Had the killer left the vehicle here knowing that the police had it on tape? The information had gone out to law enforcement departments but not the public.

Sean called the sheriff. "Let your deputies know we're here. We don't want to search the same area."

"With all that's been going on here at the station, I didn't think of that. I'll have each one call you and let you know their whereabouts."

"We'll wait until we—"

A dog barked in the distance to the left.

Sean looked in that direction. "It sounds like the dog found something."

Not a moment later, Sean received a call from Deputy Worth. "The dog found a dead body." The deputy gave Sean the location where they were.

Sean and Juan hiked southeast down the slope into the woods. Deputy Worth was on watch for them and waved his arms. When Sean arrived at the scene, he saw Deputy Simpson was there, too. Sean was surprised to see that the body belonged to the fake nurse.

Sean shook both men's hands, then moved to the dead man to assess if the murder had been committed here or the body dumped here. He lifted the guy, noting the pool of blood beneath his body from a single shot to the heart. This was where he'd been killed, then. By who? A member of the cartel? Someone not pleased with his services?

Sean stood and shifted toward the two deputies with the canine sitting between them. "Have you taken photos of the body and the surroundings?"

"Sheriff Bailey told me to back off and wait for you," Deputy Worth said.

"We'll need to search the surrounding bush for anything that might tie into this murder." Sean pointed in the direction of where the shooter must have been. "Especially that way. I think the killer was over there. Did the dog sniff the driver's seat to use as a guide to where the driver went?"

Deputy Worth nodded.

"I know the ground is mostly covered with grass and vegetation, but did either one of you see any fresh footprints?"

Deputy Worth grimaced. "I was keeping an eye on Butch. He was moving quickly, so I didn't really notice."

"I did," Simpson said. "And I only saw one set of footprints that Butch was following."

So the cleaner had been alone. Where was he going? Why was he here? "We'll take the same way back and check as we go for anything unusual, possibly widen the area. It's possible this guy was followed."

Juan moved around the body, taking photos. "Or he was meeting someone here."

"An odd place, out in the middle of nowhere." Sean felt as though the pieces of the puzzle of this case kept being rearranged. "Somebody left on a motorcycle. Most likely the killer. It's possible the motorcycle didn't come off the truck, but that the dead man was followed by the person on the motorcycle."

"Or came early and waited for the man?" Juan squatted down by the guy.

"Deputy Simpson, scour the ground near the corpse. I'll help Deputy Worth search the surroundings while you continue processing the crime scene here." Sean waved for the deputy to go to the left while he went right. "We'll start five yards out then expand the area."

After slowly circling the crime scene twice, Sean discovered a trampled area where someone had stood recently. The grass hadn't bounced back yet from being stood on. He searched the area around it to see if any clues had been left. Nothing.

Why did the cleaner come out here with another person? Or was his killer waiting for him?

Sean took photos of the ground. "Deputy Worth, we're going to try to follow the trail this person used.

Let's see if Butch can pick up the scent." He stepped back, careful not to go too near where the killer stood.

"We can try. Butch is one of the best bloodhounds at doing that."

Butch sniffed the trampled grass, indicating to Worth that there were two trails to follow. The deputy looked at Sean. "Which one?"

"Let's go away from the road and see where it leads us. We can come back and follow the other one later."

After fifteen minutes of following the bloodhound, a cabin appeared through the trees in the distance. They cautiously approached the place. Sean wasn't sure if the killer had come from here or gone here after. He tried to make a call to Juan, but cell reception didn't extend here.

He drew his gun and said in a whisper, "Let's leave Butch here while we check the cabin."

Worth nodded and removed his weapon from his holster, too.

Sean indicated that the deputy should go to the left while he went right to assess the outside from the side and back before barging in. After circling the structure, which had only one way in—the front door—Sean tried the knob, and it turned. He signaled to the deputy to go to the left again while he went right when they entered.

Sean held up one finger, two, then three—and burst into the cabin.

Aubrey sat in Sheriff Bailey's office waiting for Sean to come pick her up. She knew he was outside town running down a lead and wouldn't know that she'd shut the trial down early after the defense called their witnesses. There wasn't enough time to get closing arguments in today, so they would give those tomorrow. Then she hoped the jury would start deliberating Villa's verdict by the afternoon. The prosecutor had a solid case against Villa, but juries had surprised her in the past.

Aubrey rose and began pacing. Don had asked her to stay in his office, but she felt like a caged animal wanting to get out. Smell the fresh air. See daylight. Move freely around without worrying she could be killed.

*Father, please end this trial tomorrow. I want my family back.*

She checked her watch and sighed. Six o'clock. Where was Sean? She stared at the door, debating whether to ignore the sheriff's "request" to stay in his office or leave and get answers to all the questions swirling around in her mind. Was Sean in danger? What had been so important he had to leave town? Was Sean all right?

It always came back to that last question. She'd chewed her thumbnail, a habit she'd broken as a teenager, down to the quick, mostly in the past ninety minutes while she waited. She'd only seen Don once in that time. Was he avoiding her because something bad was going down?

She stopped in the middle of the room and drew in a deep breath, then another. She was working herself up because...

*I care about—no, I'm falling in love with Sean.*

And here she was doing the one thing she didn't want to do—waiting for the bad news concerning him.

Her shoulders drooped. She stared at the linoleum floor—a few tiles were cracked. That was how her heart felt—cracked.

As the door to the office opened, she tensed, her

hands balled at her side. She hoped it was Sean, but instead it was Texas Ranger Conde. Not a good sign. "Where's Sean?"

"He's working out of cell reception. All I know is the last time I talked to him, he went to check out the deserted black truck parked off the shoulder of a highway."

"When was that?"

"Over three hours ago."

"Isn't that a long time to be out of contact?"

"No, not if he's working a case. There are many areas in Texas that don't get cell reception. We often move in and out of it. I do know he has three men with him, so he isn't alone. There are times I get caught up in my case that I forget time."

"Yes, he does, too." Aubrey forced a smile. "I'd like to go to the safe house."

When she left the sheriff's office, Bailey was standing nearby. "See you tomorrow. When I hear from Sean, I'll have him call you."

"I appreciate that."

Don followed her and Texas Ranger Conde to the station's rear entrance, where a deputy opened the door. Jorge's car was parked as close as it could get to the exit. Three steps and she climbed into the vehicle, practically collapsing in the front seat. Her tight hold on her thoughts and body was breaking down. The past few hours had thrust her back two years while she waited to hear from her husband and never did. Instead it had been the major in Company D who had come to visit her and given her the news of his death.

When Jorge pulled into the garage at the safe house,

her cell phone rang. She dug for it in her purse and saw that it was Sean—or someone using his phone.

She quickly answered it. "Hello."

"I'm sorry I didn't let you know what was happening. I thought you would still be in the trial."

The sound of his deep voice released the tension that gripped her. "I'm glad you called, Sean." She waved for Jorge to go inside. He climbed from the car and stood at the door into the house to give her privacy.

"I called Don to let him know what we found and when you would dismiss the trial. He told me you already went to the safe house with Jorge."

"What happened?"

"I'll tell you the details later, but the good news is we found the cleaner and apparently where he'd been living, at least most recently."

"Are you bringing him in?"

"No, he's dead."

"Who killed him?" At least she wouldn't have to worry about the cleaner.

"That we don't know. That's why we're processing the scene. I'll see you in an hour or so."

"Goodbye." She put her phone back in her purse and then slid from the car.

As she walked toward Jorge, all she could think about was the new threat out there somewhere. Were there two bad guys responsible for all the things that had happened, starting with the dead rat?

Sean sat at the kitchen table with his laptop, trying to figure out who might be the mole in the police department. Jorge originally had been working from Company D headquarters on financial records of the members of the Port Bliss Police Department and had continued doing that when he became part of Aubrey's detail at the safe house. While Aubrey was in court, he worked on narrowing down any police officers living above his means. Sergeant Vic Daniels stood out, with various gambling debts that made him ripe as a candidate to be a mole.

If Cal hadn't said Vic might be the one working for the cartel, he might have overlooked him because he'd covered his tracks well, using a fake ID in an undercover operation years ago. Sean went back through the surveillance tapes to see if he could find the time Vic came around the corner, when Jana picked Cal up from work and they argued about the drawing and her cousin possibly being the fake nurse. There was a camera angled to show Vic pausing and listening to their conversation before he revealed himself as Cal and Jana were leaving.

Jorge entered the kitchen for a cup of coffee.

"Is Aubrey up yet?"

"Yes, I heard her moving around in her room. I'm not surprised she took a nap. She looked exhausted when I picked her up at the sheriff's station."

"I think I gave her a couple of gray hairs."

"That's what happens when you get caught up in a case. Just ask my wife." Jorge poured the coffee into his mug. "I'll tell Aubrey you're in here when I see her."

"Thanks. The financial records you've found on Vic will help me make the case he's the insider for the cartel."

"Good. Nothing's worse than a bad cop. Thankfully most police officers are dedicated to protecting the public."

"But when we find someone like this, it never makes

us look good." Sean sighed and leaned back in his chair, staring at the computer screen with the condemning information against Vic. Sean would show the police chief the evidence tomorrow.

Hearing a noise in the hallway, Sean glanced over his shoulder as Aubrey came into the kitchen. The sight of her always revved his heartbeat to a faster tempo. He stood and pulled out a chair for her. "Jorge said you got a good nap."

"I hadn't intended to do that. My mistake was sitting on my bed, and before I knew it I was lying down. The next thing I remember is waking up. I've had tough trials before, but this one has become personal. How long have you been here?"

"An hour." He quickly closed the laptop. Until he told Juan, he wouldn't say anything about Vic to anyone not involved in running down the information.

Aubrey sat catty-corner from him at the table. "What happened this afternoon?"

"As I told you, the guy who impersonated Chris Newton and killed him is dead. His fingerprint was found on the trunk of the car he used to transport Newton to the burial ground. He wiped his fingerprints off everywhere else but one place on the trunk. He was also involved in Cal's death."

"So he's the cleaner who was responsible for your brother's death?"

"It looks like it. As we discover the identities of all the bodies found in that field, we may be able to tie him to each crime."

"Have you figured out what his real name is?"

"Everything points to Mario Bravo, Cal's wife's cousin."

"Then he also murdered Samuel?"

"Yes, as well as his cousin Jana. It may take weeks to tie everything together, but the cabin we processed this afternoon should give us more information. We dusted everything. A lot of the prints belong to Bravo, but not all." Tomorrow Sean would meet with his informant and see if he'd heard anything else to help wrap this case up quickly. It would help Aubrey—and even him—to move on. "Another body was ID'd from the burial ground. It was the cartel lieutenant that Villa replaced."

"Villa was probably behind that death. With everything that has occurred, I want to call my children and let them know they'll be coming home soon."

"Talk to them, but don't say anything about coming home until Villa's trial is totally over. Okay?"

"But I should be able to see them by the weekend?"

"I'll personally take you there."

She smiled and cupped his hand, which rested on the table by his laptop. He looked into her eyes and felt lost in them. He was falling in love with Aubrey, but she'd made it clear she could never love a man in his line of business.

Sean walked behind an abandoned building on the outskirts of Port Bliss and leaned against the structure while he waited for his informant to appear. A man with a full beard came around the corner, his long black hair with gray sprinkled throughout it tied back in a rubber band. When he smiled, a few of his front teeth were missing, but then, what little he knew about him was that he was a boxer when he was younger.

Sean had been surprised when he'd received a hang-up from Nate this morning, which was his signal to meet. Two hang-ups in a row meant at the beach. One was here at the abandoned building. He rarely contacted him first. Usually Sean was the one who initiated it. "I was going to get in touch with you today. Why did you want to meet?"

Nate leaned against the brick structure. "Something big is going down soon."

"What?"

"The cleaner has a score to settle."

Sean relaxed his tense muscles. "We caught the cleaner yesterday."

Nate frowned. "I started hearing the rumors yesterday, but I heard more this morning. That's why I called you."

"It isn't common knowledge that we have. We're still tracking information down."

"What kind?"

"We know who he is, but he was murdered by someone right before we caught up with him."

Nate's eyes darkened, and his frown morphed into a scowl. He shook his head. "Something isn't right. No one knows who the cleaner is, except Sanchez. That's why he can move around freely. He uses disguises and blends in when he needs to. He's made quite a reputation for himself over the years."

Maybe he had it wrong about Mario Bravo, but they had him on tape driving away from Cal's house minutes after Cal had ended the call with Sean. "Was the burial ground we found the cleaner's?"

"From the rumors I've heard, yes. That's part of his ritual."

"Then hc's dcad. The news will be released soon.

The person we found was associated with the burial ground and the last person murdered there. If you still hear things about the cleaner after the information about Mario Bravo is announced, let me know." Sean shook Nate's hand.

He nodded. "I hope so. He's ruthless and heartless. A legend in the cartel."

As per their protocol, Sean slipped away first, climbed into his SUV and headed for the sheriff's office. Aubrey had texted him that the jury was deliberating Villa's verdict as of eleven o'clock this morning. Then they would move Villa to the county jail until his sentencing, if he was found guilty.

As he started his car, he received another text from Aubrey. The jury had reached a verdict. Sean increased his speed. He wanted to be there when the verdict came down and oversee Villa's transportation, if guilty. Maybe what Nate was referring to was a plan for the cartel to ambush the moving of Villa back to the county jail.

He reached the sheriff's office in record time and hurried to the room where the trial was taking place. He entered just as the jury foreman announced Villa was found guilty of first-degree murder.

Sean glanced at Aubrey. The relief in her expression smoothed out the wrinkles in her forehead. All he wanted to do was hold her and kiss away the rest of the tension that still gripped her stiff shoulders.

Villa was escorted from the room by four deputy sheriffs to await the van from the jail. As the rest of the people left, Aubrey waited for him. He made his way toward her, seeing a small smile gracing her mouth. She came around the table where she'd been sitting.

When the room was empty except for Aubrey and him, he took hold of her hands and tugged her close. "I noticed you scheduled his sentencing for Friday."

"Yes. I want to see my children this weekend and bring them home. Villa has separated me from them long enough."

He smoothed her hair behind her ear. "I'll let my sister know we'll be driving up there to get them on Saturday. Okay?"

"No private plane this time?"

He shook his head. "Only because they'll be safe."

"Well, in that case I'll manage the thirteen-hour trip to get them."

And it would give them time to talk. He didn't want to end what was developing between them.

"I want to follow the van to the county jail. I'll feel better when he goes inside. I can come back and pick you up."

"Sounds like a good plan."

Don stuck his head into the room. "The van is here."

"Okay. I'm coming." Sean squeezed Aubrey's hand gently then released it.

"Two of my deputies will be in the front while two will be riding in back with Villa. I'll be in front of the van," Don said.

"And I'll be following them." Sean smiled at Aubrey as he made his way to the door to go outside and check the area with Don before the deputies and Villa left by the rear entrance. Sean and the sheriff scanned the buildings around the station, but Sean didn't see anything suspicious. If the cartel tried to help Villa escape, it would be en route to the county jail. There were several ways to travel there. The sheriff in the lead car would make the decision which one he would take.

While Don was on one side and Sean the other, the deputies brought Villa out and safely put him into the van.

Sean headed for his SUV, breathing a little easier for the moment. He couldn't let down his guard. His job was to take up the rear and prevent anyone coming up from behind to hijack the van.

Sean arrived last at the prison, where the deputies were already taking Villa out of the van. They were supposed to wait until he and Don assessed the surroundings, although the county jail was off by itself right outside town.

Sean slammed to a halt and jumped out of his SUV. "Wait!"

In that second a bullet struck Villa in the middle of his forehead—a kill shot. He collapsed to the ground as Sean grabbed his rifle and tried to calculate where the shot came from.

The clock tower? It was the only structure with the right trajectory. He hopped back into his SUV and sped away from the van toward the tower. Whoever had just killed Villa was an expert shot. The distance meant it was a person trained as a sniper.

He pressed his foot harder on the accelerator, keeping an eye on the only escape from the tower. In the thirty seconds it took him to get in his SUV and drive away from the crime scene, no one had come out of the door. Was his informant right about Mario Bravo not being the cleaner? Or was there a new one sent by Sanchez?

His car came to a screeching halt near the tall tower's only entrance. He shoved open his door, drawing his Sig Sauer P226 pistol from his holster while he rushed into the slender, tall building. The quiet taunted him. He took the stairs, checking any place a person could squeeze into and hide. When he reached the top, he spun slowly around. No one was there but him. Was he wrong in his estimation of the killer's whereabouts?

Then his gaze latched onto a rope thrown out of a wide window-like opening that afforded a sweeping view of Port Bliss and the water between the mainland and South Padre Island. He covered the distance to it and leaned out of the opening. In the distance, a slender person dressed in black jumped on a motorcycle and disappeared over a hill. He started to turn to hurry back to his car when a splotch of red on the rope caught his full attention. Blood? Then he spied a jagged piece of rock siding nearby with red on it, too.

He called Don and asked him to track the motorcycle with a person in black with a sniper rifle slung across his back. Sean snapped photos of the evidence then took out his knife and cut the rope. He pulled it up and wound it in a circle, seeing various other red spots on the twine.

At least he had DNA of the killer. He hoped it led to a person's name.

Aubrey stood in front of the bay window in the safe house kitchen, staring at an empty backyard where she tried to imagine her children playing and laughing like they had at home. Jorge had brought her back because Don and Sean were tracking a sniper who'd killed Villa. The situation again put Sean in harm's way. She had to halt her growing feelings for Sean. She just couldn't go through another loved one dying in the line of fire. He loved being a protector, but at the same time, that trait could cause an early death.

The sound of the front door opening then closing

caused Aubrey to twist around to face the entrance into the kitchen. Footfalls drew closer, and seconds later, Sean appeared in the room. The haggard look on his face tugged at her. No, she needed to keep her distance and keep her walls up.

"Did you catch the sniper?" she finally asked.

"No, he disappeared, but we're analyzing the blood on a rope that he used to escape the clock tower."

"What if he isn't in the system?"

"I choose to believe he will be. We'll know something by tomorrow morning. We discovered the weapon that killed Villa also killed your husband and some of the ones at the burial ground who were murdered by a gun."

"How about Cal when he was in my backyard?"

"The bullet didn't come from that gun or the one that Mario Bravo had on him when we found him. But the sniper could have several guns he uses."

So much information to keep track of. A dull headache thudded against her forehead. "I want to bring my children home, but I can't as long as that person is out there. We don't have any idea what his agenda is." She blew out a loud breath. "I was hoping after Villa was sentenced, I could be with Sammy and Camy."

"Let's see what happens with the DNA test being rushed through. I have a feeling things will come together. We've learned a lot in the past weeks." Sean closed the distance between them.

"So Mario Bravo didn't kill Samuel, but this unknown sniper did."

"Technically the gun the sniper used killed Samuel. That doesn't mean the sniper did, but I think he did. To a sniper, a gun is important."

Aubrey massaged her fingers against her temples. "I'm on overload. I've eaten dinner and left you some in the refrigerator to heat up. I'm going to bed. Tomorrow I'm going to my office at the courthouse. I need to finish the paperwork on Villa's trial." She started to move around him.

Sean touched her arm, the space between them narrowing. "I know how hard this has been for you, especially concerning your family."

"I'd worked through my grief over Samuel's death, then all this started happening and I'm having to go through it again while keeping my family safe." *Then you go after a sniper who just killed Villa.* "I want a life without this kind of conflict. My children deserve not to worry about what might happen to me."

"I understand what you're going through. I stared down at Jack's decomposed body in a grave. All the pain I'd been trying to push away came like a slamming fist to my gut. I owe it to Jack and Samuel to solve their murders."

"So that's why you went after the sniper by yourself with no backup. From what I heard, the sniper was really good. Villa was shot right between the eyes. He could have shot you while you were trying to get to him."

"But he didn't, because he was escaping. That was more important to him. The sniper has to be stopped, or he'll keep killing others. There have to be people who'll do that, or lawlessness will prevail."

"I know." *Just not you.* She looked into his eyes and saw the hurt there. For a few seconds she thought she and Sean had a chance… "I'm going to bed. Good night, Sean."

She practically ran from the kitchen. She loved him, but she couldn't go through what had happened with Samuel again with Sean.

"Thanks, Don. I'm not surprised, but it's good to have it confirmed. Have we got any results back about the blood on the rope?" Sean asked the next morning as he left the safe house with Aubrey, who was going to work at the reopened courthouse. He slanted a look at her. She faced forward, but she stared out the window. "The DNA from the blood on the coverlet is Jana Adams's. The question is who killed her, Mario Bravo or the person who killed him?"

"Does it make any difference? She's another person who's been murdered. Another family will be mourning."

"I know the past two weeks have been horrific, but at the least the discovery of the bodies in the burial ground will allow their families to have closure. That's important."

She finally swung her attention to him. "I'm sorry. I know that means a lot to those families. You're one of them. I just need to hold my children. We've never been apart for long. I used to think I was tough. After all, I'm a judge and have overseen many felony trials. I had to ID my husband. I saw firsthand a brutal murderer's work." She returned to focusing on the landscape going by.

Silence ruled.

Sean pulled into the rear parking lot at the courthouse near the sidewalk into the building. He got out at the same time as Aubrey and they walked to the entrance. When Aubrey saw Bill on guard at the door, her solemn expression transformed into a smile.

"I'm so glad you're all right, Bill."

The deputy sheriff blushed. "I was in the hospital overnight, but I'm fine. Just a mild concussion and a flesh wound that bled more than it should have."

"You shouldn't be back on duty so quickly."

Bill chuckled. "Judge Madison, I seem to remember you coming back too fast just last week."

"That's because I needed to get the Villa trial over with before too many people got hurt."

Bill leaned toward her and murmured, "It's been extra quiet around here this morning. All trials have been postponed until tomorrow."

"Good. Others won't interrupt me, and I can get caught up on paperwork."

Sean scanned the area. "Deputy Lockhart, are the tight protocols being maintained?"

"Yes, there'll be two guards back here tomorrow when the trials start again."

"See you later," Aubrey said and headed for the front of the courthouse.

Sean followed. "Where are you going? The stairs are back there."

"I'm using the front stairs. Too many bad memories of being trapped in that stairwell." In a quieter voice she added, "I thought I was going to die in it."

"What happened a couple of days ago isn't the usual."

She didn't say anything.

At her office, Sean greeted the guard at her door then went in first to check the room. A few minutes later he came out into the hallway. "It's clear. I'll pick you up at twelve unless you want to go earlier. Call if so."

She nodded and entered her chambers, shutting the door behind her.

Sean first drove to the police station. He needed to talk with Juan about Sergeant Vic Daniels. The police chief greeted Sean with a handshake.

"How's the manhunt for Villa's killer going?"

"Slow. My description of the sniper wasn't exactly that revealing. Slender and about five foot seven or eight isn't much to go on. He was covered in black from head to toe. Can't even tell you what color his hair was. It was under a hoodie. I didn't get a good look at the motorcycle, either. I saw him disappearing over the rise. It wasn't a hog but more like a medium-sized bike."

"That's more than half the ones I see around here."

"Can we go into your office?"

"Sure." Juan moved toward it.

Sean closed the door behind them. "I believe I've found the mole in your department. I've been checking financial records, and this officer is spending money way over his income."

"Who?"

"Vic Daniels. A lot of stuff he bought was with cash. Something is fishy. Also, I know Cal thought he could have been a mole because he overheard Vic and his wife discussing that her cousin was the cleaner. Since then we think Mario Bravo was the cleaner or working with him." Sean gave him a full report on his findings concerning Daniels.

"Thanks, and I mean it. The idea of one of my officers being a mole for the cartel is unacceptable. Working as a law enforcement officer is hard enough without having a traitor in our midst."

"If I can help, I will."

"Keep digging for more information. I will, too. I don't want anyone else working on this."

"I agree. The pattern I uncovered is over three years old."

"Which makes you wonder if he had a role in your brother's death? The sergeant was the investigator for Jack's case."

"I won't deny that. It's something I've considered, but it also means I'll make sure whoever is the mole is revealed. If something comes up, call me." Sean left Juan's office and hurried toward the exit. In the parking lot, he spied Vic driving away from the police station.

At the moment, the more important issue he needed to investigate was who killed Villa. He headed to the sheriff's office. The instant he arrived and stepped into the station, Sean knew something big was going down. He crossed to Don, who was talking with several of his deputies.

"We've got the sniper's photo. We need to release this information across the country since it's been a day since she killed Villa. She could be anywhere." The sheriff passed out photos to his people.

*She?* When Don gave him the picture, then signaled they go into the sheriff's office, Sean followed and closed the door. "Jana Adams isn't dead. She's the sniper?"

"The DNA matches. Did she kill her husband? Her cousin? Why? What's going on here?"

"All good questions, and I don't have answers. We have the black truck leaving at the time of Cal's death.

We only saw one body in the cab—a large person around six feet. Jana Adams isn't that tall."

Sean rubbed the back of his neck. "If Jana is a sniper, where did she come from? We need to dig into her background. Check into her family in Houston. Plus we need to get her photo out to the media. Give me a computer, and I can start now. I don't have to pick up Aubrey for a couple of hours."

"You can use my office. I'll get you a laptop."

While Don slipped out of the room, Sean prowled the small area, feeling caged. Many questions were still left unanswered. He'd met Jana, and she hadn't seemed like a sniper, which might be why she was so successful.

Aubrey stared out the window. Sean had called and said he'd be there at noon. The church bells rang every day at that time. She grabbed her purse and headed down the front stairs. There were only a few people at the courthouse. That seemed strange to her. Usually there was a lot of activity, but without trials taking place, the numbers were way down.

She walked down the long hall, greeting Bill with a smile. "How's it been this morning?"

"Quiet, which is nice after the past couple of weeks." He opened the door for her.

"Thanks. Today is a beautiful day."

"Is your ride here?"

She checked her watch. "Yes, it's noon."

Aubrey exited the building, pausing a few seconds to relish the light breeze and the warmth of the sun on a gorgeous day. It lifted her spirits.

Halfway down the sidewalk to the parking lot, Aubrey spied Sergeant Daniels coming her way. A grim expression darkened his features. Bad news?

He stopped in front of her. "Judge, you need to come with me. There's been a development—"

A shot rang out at almost the same time as the sergeant's eyes rounded. A bullet pierced her shoulder. Vic fell forward into her. She staggered backward as his weight finally took her down.

On the way to pick up Aubrey, Sean received a call from the sheriff. He punched his answer button on his steering wheel. "What's up, Don?"

"We got a tip that a woman who fit the description of Jana Adams has been sighted near the courthouse. I'm calling Juan next."

"Good. Let your deputies there know about the sighting. I'm almost there." He disconnected the call and pressed his foot on the accelerator. He didn't want to put on his siren and spook Jana into running.

As he turned into the rear parking lot, he heard a shot and glimpsed Daniels stumbling into...Aubrey. She fell with the sergeant on top of her.

*No! Not Aubrey!*

Deputy Lockhart, along with two other deputies, ran toward Aubrey and Daniels. Sean slammed on his brakes, checking the line of fire. The only possible place was the hospital's roof. He moved toward Aubrey as he called Juan to send police officers to the Port Bliss Hospital. Then he hurried to Aubrey as Lockhart and another deputy dragged Daniels off her.

The sight of her on the ground, blood flowing from her shoulder, spurred Sean faster. As he ran, he called

911 to report two people down. When he reached Aubrey's side, he knelt.

"We need to get out of the range of the sniper," he shouted at the deputies.

Lockhart checked Daniels's pulse. "He's dead."

"Aubrey, I'm moving you into the building." He slid his arms under her, being careful not to jostle her right shoulder. As he quickly moved to the entrance, Lockhart ran ahead to open the door.

Inside the building, Sean carefully laid Aubrey on the floor out of the range of the sniper.

"Sean—get the guy." Her gaze, filled with pain, linked with his. "We can't—live always in fear. Go."

"There was only that one shot. There may be more. I need to protect you."

"Go. Bill's here."

Sean didn't want to, and yet he did because Aubrey was right.

Bill waved his hand. "I'll take care of her."

Sean rose, wishing he could be in two places at the same time. As he exited the building, he raced for his SUV. On the way to the hospital only three blocks away, he called Juan. "What's going on? Did you catch Jana?"

"No. But we've locked down the hospital. There's no way she got out. We had two officers at the hospital in the ER. They moved into action right away."

"I'm almost there." He tore out of the parking lot. With the hospital locked down, he needed to find Jana fast before she killed others. And Aubrey needed to be treated at the ER.

When he arrived, a dozen officers were making their way into the hospital. After thinking about how she escaped from the clock tower, Sean instead started circling the building. At the rear, he found a rope dangling down from the roof, but it fell short by seven feet. Underneath the rope, a small bush was stomped into the ground as though a body had fallen on it.

Since he didn't see her as he rounded the hospital, he kept going, assessing his surroundings as he went. About fifteen yards away, he saw someone dressed in jeans, a jacket and a ball cap pulled down low. He quickened his step as the person limped as fast as she— Jana—could.

He spied the motorcycle another twenty yards away from her, and he flat out ran. She turned, drew a handgun from her jacket pocket.

He stopped, planted his feet and raised his weapon. "Drop the gun."

She lifted it and aimed it at him at the same time he pulled the trigger.

Drowsy, Aubrey opened her eyes to a hospital room. Not the same one she'd been in nearly two weeks ago. For a few moments she tried to remember why she was here. Sergeant Daniels stood in front of her—then fell forward against her. She touched her right shoulder, feeling the bandage under her fingertips.

The last thing she remembered was Sean carrying her inside. He wanted to stay. She told him to go after the sniper. She couldn't believe she had said that to him. What if something happened to him because of her? She loved him. No matter what job he had, that wasn't going to change.

The door opened. She tensed, remembering the time when the fake nurse came into her room.

But instead, it was the most beautiful sight to her

eyes. Sean, tired, worried, closed the space between them. "The doctor said you're going to be all right." He sat in the chair by the bed and took her hand. "I'm so sorry I was late picking you up."

"You weren't. Did you get the sniper? Is this over with?"

He smiled. "Yes. The sniper was Jana Adams. She's hurt and in the hospital right now, but well guarded. She wasn't after you. She came after Vic for trying to kill her husband. He was the one who shot Cal in your backyard. Vic was the mole for the cartel in the police department."

"Who was the cleaner?"

"Both Mario Bravo and Jana. They were cousins and worked together until Bravo killed Cal, because he's the one who knew that Bravo was the fake nurse and killed the real Chris Newton. Jana didn't think Cal would keep that a secret."

"So Jana really loved her husband?"

"Yes, that's why she pretended she was kidnapped so Cal would stay quiet. Bravo didn't want him around at all. It gave her time to try to get rid of Bravo."

"What about all that blood on the coverlet?"

"She always had a plan to get away clean with everyone thinking she was dead. She had some of her blood kept in the refrigerator at the house in the woods. She has volunteered to testify against Sanchez and the top people in the Coastal Cartel, although she will serve time."

"So much violence. At least our loved ones' murderer was either captured or dead. Finally, closure." Aubrey closed her eyes and drew in several deep breaths.

"I love you, Aubrey."

Her eyes flew open. His words sent her heart beating rapidly.

"I know my job is a huge barrier for you. I—"

She put two fingers over his lips. "I love you. I want to see if we can work something out. We both went through a lot with this case. We need time to figure our relationship out."

He leaned close to her and kissed her. "You can have all the time you need. My love isn't going away."

# EPILOGUE

*Eighteen months later*

"Mama! Mama, they're here." Sammy ran into the kitchen.

"Then you need to greet your guests. It's not every day a boy turns six years old. It'll be great having your friends and Camy's here at the ranch for your birthday party."

Aubrey's mother came into the room. "There you are. You've got visitors, Sammy."

Her son whirled around and raced out of the kitchen, nearly running into Sean. "Gotta go," Sammy said and charged down the hall.

"And I'd better go and make sure he doesn't mow down any of his friends in his enthusiasm." Her mother left as Aubrey's husband entered.

Sean chuckled. "I'd like to borrow half his energy." He stopped in front of her and put his arms loosely around her. "How's the food coming?"

Aubrey grinned. "You know better than to ask me that. Remember, Mama is the cook, not me. The caterer is down at the barn getting everything set up for the party."

"And the horses are ready for the kids to ride. My job is done for the day. Now I get to sit back and enjoy my family having fun."

Aubrey snuggled closer. "I'm not sure Sammy and Camy are going to have the most fun. It just might be me. You've planned every detail of this birthday party."

"That's because you went into town to see a client in jail."

Since moving to Amarillo, she'd been working part-time for an organization that offered people who couldn't afford an attorney the services of a lawyer. She loved the work. It gave her a chance to spend more time with her children, too.

"Do you regret coming back here to run your family's ranch?" she asked.

He bent forward and kissed her. "Not one bit. The time I spent in law enforcement was important to me, but I've always loved this ranch, too. I had wonderful memories of this place, and I want our children to have that, too."

Aubrey felt her baby kick. She placed Sean's hand on her rounded stomach. "Speaking of our children, feel him. He's been active today. He liked what you said."

Awe showed in Sean's eyes. "He's going to be like Sammy. Poor Camy."

"Camy will be able to hold her own with her two brothers. She outrides Sammy, who isn't too happy about that. But my son will have to learn everyone has strengths and weaknesses."

Sean framed Aubrey's face with his hands. "You are a wise woman. Do you miss being a judge?"

"No. I'm helping people, not judging them. I didn't realize how much I would like that." After the Villa trial, it didn't take her long to realize that Sean was too ingrained in her life for her to walk away from him. "You're the one who taught me to give my trust to the Lord and to let go of worrying. It has freed me. That's one of the many reasons I love you."

"And you taught me to live again and not blame myself for what happened to Jack. You're my other half." His mouth settled over hers.

\* \* \* \* \*

*If you loved this exciting romantic suspense, pick up the other books in Margaret Daley's Lone Star Justice miniseries:*

High-Risk Reunion
Lone Star Christmas Rescue
Texas Ranger Showdown
Texas Baby Pursuit
Lone Star Christmas Witness

*Available now from Love Inspired Suspense!*

*Find more great reads at www.LoveInspired.com*

Dear Reader,

This is the sixth book in the Lone Star Justice series. I had fun writing the twins—Sammy and Camy. They were my lightness in the middle of a dark story about drugs pouring into our country. Aubrey went through a lot in her life as a mother, wife and judge. She didn't want to fall in love with Sean and end up losing him like she did her husband, Samuel. Love is a strong emotion, but so is fear. Fear keeps you from doing something you want to do or should do. She had to learn to turn her fear over to the Lord in order to fall in love again.

I love hearing from readers. You can email me at *margaretdaley@gmail.com* and join my monthly newsletter by signing up on the front page of my website, www.margaretdaley.com. Also on my website you can see what books are out and coming soon, as well as links to them.

Take care,

Margaret Daley

COMING NEXT MONTH FROM
## Love Inspired® Suspense

Available June 4, 2019

### BLIND TRUST
*True Blue K-9 Unit* • by Laura Scott
When guide dog trainer Eva Kendall stumbles on a dognapping, she
quickly learns *she's* the ultimate target. But can officer Finn Gallagher
and his K-9 partner, Abernathy, help her track down the puppy she's
training...and uncover why someone's set their deadly sights on her?

### LONE WITNESS
*FBI: Special Crimes Unit* • by Shirlee McCoy
Rescuing a little girl from a kidnapping thrusts Tessa Carlson from her
hideout into the media's spotlight—and a killer's crosshairs. But the
child's father, widowed FBI agent Henry Miller, vows he'll protect her
from the ruthless criminal who wants her dead.

### GUARDING THE AMISH MIDWIFE
*Amish Country Justice* • by Dana R. Lynn
On the way to deliver her cousin's baby, Amish midwife Lizzy Miller
witnesses her driver's murder—and now someone plans to silence her.
Lizzy knows better than to trust strangers, but her very survival depends
on the help of former Amish man turned police officer Isaac Yoder.

### DANGER ON THE RANCH
*Roughwater Ranch Cowboys* • by Dana Mentink
After her serial killer ex-husband escapes from prison, Jane Reyes has
only one person to turn to—his brother who put him in jail. But when
she shows up at Mitch Whitehorse's ranch, can he keep Jane and the
nephew he never knew about safe?

### HIDDEN TWIN
by Jodie Bailey
Amy Brady has been in witness protection for three years when
someone threatens her life—and her twin's. Now it's US marshal
Samuel Maldonado's duty to get her to safety. But if she ever hopes to be
reunited with her sister, Amy must work with Sam to expose a murderer.

### PERILOUS PURSUIT
by Kathleen Tailer
Someone will do anything to get Mackenzie Weaver's documentary
footage—even kill her. But US deputy marshal Jake Riley won't let
anyone harm his late best friend's little sister...especially since he's
beginning to wish they could have a future together.

LOOK FOR THESE AND OTHER LOVE INSPIRED BOOKS WHEREVER
BOOKS ARE SOLD, INCLUDING MOST BOOKSTORES, SUPERMARKETS,
DISCOUNT STORES AND DRUGSTORES.

LISCNM0519

# Get 4 FREE REWARDS!

## We'll send you 2 FREE Books plus 2 FREE Mystery Gifts.

**Love Inspired® Suspense** books feature Christian characters facing challenges to their faith... and lives.

**FREE** Value Over **$20**

---

**YES!** Please send me 2 FREE Love Inspired® Suspense novels and my 2 FREE mystery gifts (gifts are worth about $10 retail). After receiving them, if I don't wish to receive any more books, I can return the shipping statement marked "cancel." If I don't cancel, I will receive 4 brand-new novels every month and be billed just $5.24 each for the regular-print edition or $5.74 each for the larger-print edition in the U.S., or $5.74 each for the regular-print edition or $6.24 each for the larger-print edition in Canada. That's a savings of at least 13% off the cover price. It's quite a bargain! Shipping and handling is just 50¢ per book in the U.S. and 75¢ per book in Canada.* I understand that accepting the 2 free books and gifts places me under no obligation to buy anything. I can always return a shipment and cancel at any time. The free books and gifts are mine to keep no matter what I decide.

Choose one: ☐ **Love Inspired® Suspense**
Regular-Print
(153/353 IDN GMY5)

☐ **Love Inspired® Suspense**
Larger-Print
(107/307 IDN GMY5)

Name (please print)

Address      Apt. #

City      State/Province      Zip/Postal Code

### Mail to the Reader Service:
**IN U.S.A.:** P.O. Box 1341, Buffalo, NY 14240-8531
**IN CANADA:** P.O. Box 603, Fort Erie, Ontario L2A 5X3

**Want to try 2 free books from another series?** Call 1-800-873-8635 or visit www.ReaderService.com.

---

*Terms and prices subject to change without notice. Prices do not include sales taxes, which will be charged (if applicable) based on your state or country of residence. Canadian residents will be charged applicable taxes. Offer not valid in Quebec. This offer is limited to one order per household. Books received may not be as shown. Not valid for current subscribers to Love Inspired Suspense books. All orders subject to approval. Credit or debit balances in a customer's account(s) may be offset by any other outstanding balance owed by or to the customer. Please allow 4 to 6 weeks for delivery. Offer available while quantities last.

**Your Privacy**—The Reader Service is committed to protecting your privacy. Our Privacy Policy is available online at www.ReaderService.com or upon request from the Reader Service. We make a portion of our mailing list available to reputable third parties that offer products we believe may interest you. If you prefer that we not exchange your name with third parties, or if you wish to clarify or modify your communication preferences, please visit us at www.ReaderService.com/consumerschoice or write to us at Reader Service Preference Service, P.O. Box 9062, Buffalo, NY 14240-9062. Include your complete name and address.

LIS19R

SPECIAL EXCERPT FROM

*Love Inspired.*
SUSPENSE

*When a guide-dog trainer becomes a target of a
dangerous crime ring, a K-9 cop and his loyal
partner will work together to keep her safe.*

*Read on for a sneak preview of*
Blind Trust *by Laura Scott,
the next exciting installment in the
True Blue K-9 Unit miniseries, available
June 2019 from Love Inspired Suspense.*

Eva Kendall slowed her pace as she approached the training facility where she worked training guide dogs.

Using her key, she entered the training center, thinking about the male chocolate Lab named Cocoa that she would work with this morning. Cocoa was a ten-week-old puppy born to Stella, a gift from the Czech Republic to the NYC K-9 Command Unit located in Queens. Most of Stella's pups were being trained as police dogs, but not Cocoa. In less than a month after basic puppy training, Cocoa would be able to go home with Eva to be fostered during his initial first-year training to become a full-fledged guide dog. Once that year passed, guide dogs like Cocoa would return to the center to train with their new owners.

A few steps into the building, Eva frowned at the loud thumps interspersed between a cacophony of barking. The raucous noise from the various canines contained a level of panic and fear rather than excitement.

Concerned, she moved quickly through the dimly lit training center to the back hallway, where the kennels were located. Normally she was the first one in every morning, but maybe one of the other trainers had gotten an early start.

Rounding the corner, she paused in the doorway when she saw a tall, heavyset stranger scooping Cocoa out of his kennel. Panic squeezed her chest. "Hey! What are you doing?"

The ferocious barking increased in volume, echoing off the walls and ceiling. The stranger must have heard her. He turned to look at her, then roughly tucked Cocoa under his arm like a football.

"No! Stop!" Panicked, Eva charged toward the man, desperately wishing she had a weapon of some sort.

"Get out of my way," he said in a guttural voice.

"No. Put that puppy down right now!" Eva stopped and stood her ground.

"Last chance," he taunted, coming closer.

*Don't miss*
Blind Trust *by Laura Scott,*
*available June 2019 wherever*
Love Inspired® Suspense *books and ebooks are sold.*

www.LoveInspired.com

Copyright © 2019 by Harlequin Books S.A.

LISEXP0519

Looking for inspiration in tales
of hope, faith and heartfelt romance?

Check out **Love Inspired**® and
**Love Inspired**® **Suspense** books!

**New books available every month!**

---

**CONNECT WITH US AT:**

Facebook.com/groups/HarlequinConnection

Facebook.com/HarlequinBooks

Twitter.com/HarlequinBooks

Instagram.com/HarlequinBooks

Pinterest.com/HarlequinBooks

ReaderService.com

LIGENRE2018R2

## SPECIAL EXCERPT FROM

*Laura Beth is determined to leave Cedar Grove to find love and start a family, but then an Englischer and his baby are stranded on her property. Could her greatest wish be right in front of her?*

*Read on for a sneak preview of*
The Wish *by Patricia Davids*
*available May 2019 from HQN Books!*

"What is that?" Laura Beth Yoder wondered out loud.

She stepped out onto the porch and folded her arms tightly across her chest. She closed her eyes and turned her head slightly, waiting for a break in the sound of the storm. There it was again.

It was a car horn. She was sure of it. Was someone in trouble? Lifting a raincoat from the hook by the door, Laura Beth pulled it on and zipped it up to her chin. She walked out onto the end of the porch.

Was she really going out into this storm? Whenever the wind died a little, she heard the horn again. It sounded like it was coming from the bridge.

The sight that met her eyes when she reached the top of the lane sent her heart hammering in terror.

A car had plowed into the rocky embankment of the creek at the edge of the bridge. The floodwaters swirling under it would continue to rise. They were already at the bottom of the car doors.

A dark-haired man sat slumped over the steering wheel. Blood trickled from his temple.

"Mister, you need to get out!"

He slowly raised a hand to the side of his head and blinked. She pulled on the door handle. It was locked. "You have to get out."

A high-pitched wail came from inside. She shone her light in the back seat. A baby sat strapped into a car seat. Water was already seeping inside the vehicle. She yanked on the rear door handle, but it was locked, too. The car shifted again. How long before the floodwaters swept them away? Was she going to watch this innocent child die?

She pulled on the door with all her might. It wouldn't budge.

She'd never felt more alone and powerless. Fighting down her panic, she searched for a way to break the glass. She hurried to shore, found a large rock and returned to the car. Praying the glass wouldn't injure the child, she closed her eyes and slammed the stone against the window.

*Don't miss*
The Wish *by Patricia Davids,*
*available May 2019 wherever*
*HQN Books and ebooks are sold.*

www.Harlequin.com

Copyright © 2019 by Patricia MacDonald

## Inspirational Romance to Warm Your Heart and Soul

Join our social communities to connect with other readers who share your love!

Sign up for the Love Inspired newsletter at **www.LoveInspired.com** to be the first to find out about upcoming titles, special promotions and exclusive content.

**CONNECT WITH US AT:**

Facebook.com/groups/HarlequinConnection

 Facebook.com/LoveInspiredBooks

 Twitter.com/LoveInspiredBks

LISOCIAL2018